Henry Martin Walker

**The Loves which Reign in the Heart of Mary**

Henry Martin Walker

**The Loves which Reign in the Heart of Mary**

ISBN/EAN: 9783337377069

Printed in Europe, USA, Canada, Australia, Japan

Cover: Foto ©Andreas Hilbeck / pixelio.de

More available books at **www.hansebooks.com**

OUR LADY'S LIBRARY.

Convent of the Maternal Heart of Mary.

# THE LOVES WHICH REIGN

### IN THE

# HEART OF MARY.

### FOR

# Our Lady's true Lovers,

### SHOWING

HOW THEY MAY INCREASE THEIR LOVE,
AND LIVE IN STILL CLOSER UNION WITH THEIR
SWEET MOTHER, BY STUDYING THE EMANA-
TIONS OF HER PURE HEART.

## FOR THE MONTH OF MAY;

AND COULD BE USED WITH PROFIT ANY
MONTH OF THE YEAR.

London:

THOMAS RICHARDSON AND SON,

AND DERBY.

[*And may be had at the Convent of the Maternal
Heart of Mary, Hyson Green, Nottingham.*]

# Imprimatur.

## ✠ EDUARDUS,

### Episcopus Nottinghamiensis.

Die 2 Aprilis, 1882.

St. Barnabas's Cathedral,
Nottingham.

We have read the book entitled
"THE LOVES WHICH REIGN IN THE
HEART OF MARY" with much interest
and edification. The author draws a
lovely picture of the pure and loving
dispositions of the Mother of God, of
her who was "a lily among thorns."
The contemplation of her beautiful
virtues will be a great help to all the
children of Mary, and will be prized
especially by those who have given
themselves wholly to her as her very
own, to be moulded in all things in
her likeness. We highly approve and
recommend this little work.

✠ EDWARD,
BISHOP OF NOTTINGHAM.

# PREFACE.

—:o:—

There is not much to be said by way of preface to this little work. It will stand very well on its own merits, and needs no additional recommendation beyond the approval of lawful authority. It is to be hoped that it will produce the fruit the pious authoress had in view in writing it, viz., a great increase of love and devotion to the Holy Mother of God. It may perhaps induce its readers to make themselves acquainted with the other little works of the same series, "OUR LADY'S LIBRARY."

The title, "THE LOVES WHICH REIGN IN THE HEART OF MARY," has, I believe, been objected to by some: but it is not easy to find another more suitable, or which better expresses the character of the work. There is, perhaps, in some minds, what may be called a kind of pious prudery, which however is anything but pious, and which does not deserve concessions, or even recognition. The holy name of the Mother of God will, it is to be hoped, be a sufficient shield and protection to prevent the words " The Loves of the Heart of Mary" from suggesting aught but what is holy. At least it may be said, if defence is needed, that there are many expressions in the popular writings of Saints, such as St. Francis of Sales, St. Bernardine of Sienna, St. Alphonsus Liguori, and others, which such a tone of mind as that alluded to would consider highly objectionable.

The maxim, "likes are cured by likes" (similia similibus curantur), whether true or not in medical science, has certainly a true meaning in the science of the Saints. It was, in a very great measure, their tender, enthusiastic, burning love for the holy Virgin Mother of God which made saints the angels in human flesh that they were. And never was such a remedy more needed than in these sad days in which we live. Hear, for instance, (to quote only two examples out of a multitude) the Blessed John Berchmans exclaiming, as he constantly did, " I will never rest till I have obtained a tender love for Mary my Mother." Hear the great modern Doctor of the Church, St. Alphonsus, serenading, as one might call it, his Heavenly Queen, in those sweet hymns of his, translated and published by the Redemptorist Fathers; for example :—

" I am the lover of a Queen,
  Whose heart so sweet and kind doth prove,
  That seeing one who seeks her love
She scouts him not, though poor and mean.

" This Virgin is so pure that she
  Was chosen by the Eternal Word,
  The Spouse and Mother of my Lord,
And she has stolen my heart from me.

" Then, Mary, stretch thy hand to me,
  Sweet loving robber seize thy prey ;
  Take from my breast this heart away
That sighs and languishes for thee."

Or hear him again pouring forth his affection with such prayer as this, which is one instance out of a thousand :—

"O most beautiful, most holy, most amiable, sweetest creature in the world: I rejoice in thy happiness; I love thee, and I hope always to love thee, both in time and in eternity."—*Glories of Mary,* p. 192.

The words of God are ever being fulfilled: "I will put enmities between thee (the serpent) and the woman, and thy seed and her seed. She shall crush thy head, and thou shalt lie in wait for her heel."

By the same way that man fell, by that way, inversely, will he be recovered from the effects of the fall. As Eve was the primary occasion of our ruin, so is Mary of our restoration :—

" Sumens illud Ave
Mutans Hevæ nomen."

H. M. W.

Kenilworth.

# CONTENTS.

—:-O-:—

# INTRODUCTION.

It is now some seven years ago since the little "Message for the Month of May" made its appearance. Its object was to show the yearning of the Mother-Heart of Mary for children; to show how ardently that sweet Mother longs for souls to form and fashion to the likeness of Jesus; how she desires to perform again her motherly offices to our dear Lord in the person of His members; to have souls so entirely her own, so given to her, that she may renew again the joy of her Heart,— that mother-joy that only mothers know, (we mean mothers in the supernatural as well as in the natural order.) We said in the little work to which we are referring, that "God, even God, after the possession of Himself, could give Mary no greater joy than to give her children."

The little book, together with the "Path of Mary," went forth: it did its work. Holy guardian angels led their clients into this sweet way of Mary. They have thanked God again and again for the great grace He vouch-

1

safed them in making known to them this precious "secret." They value it more now than when they first heard of it, and yet still, as we have told them, there are beauties still unknown, grand graces still hidden. The Venerable de Montfort speaks of the graces of the first step, second step, third step, and still more the supremely happy, saintly soul who, neither turning to right or left, makes this wonderful devotion its habitual state, and is daily advancing step by step, until the final step is taken to the feet of Mary in heaven.* God grant us grace to persevere, that we may attain this happy end.

To look at matters in a general light does not avail much; we must descend into particulars to find out whether we are advancing as we should be, whether the consecration we have made of ourselves to Mary was only a formal act, never really carried into effect; whether we may not be Mary's own in name only, as many Christians are Christian in name only, and do not correspond to the grand title they bear, and which they would be sorry to lose, as we should be to lose our claim upon our own dear Mother by the title we bear of her very own, in consequence of the

* See "The Secret of Mary," by the Venerable de Montfort.

offering we have made of our whole beings to
her. Therefore this little work is written to
help those on their way to Mary, who may be
at a standstill, to draw them nearer to her, to
enkindle greater love, to bring them closer,
and make them dearer to the Mother of fair
love, who is so anxious her children should
walk ever in her company, and is afraid of
their straying far off, for fear they should fall
into the tempter's snares.

How should we keep near to our Mother?
What will draw us close to her? Come near
and see. Lay your head upon her bosom.
There is a warm Heart of love beneath that
dear breast of Mary. Its every beating is
sweet to the ears of God; every pulsation of
the pure blood within that dear human Heart
is as a strain of lovely music to God,—and
why? Because it is, and it ever was, instinct
with all that is beautiful, all that is holy,
loving, generous, entirely lost in love for God
and man. Such is our Mother's Heart; and if
we draw close, and place our own hearts close
to hers, and learn its loves, and in our measure
love its loves, we too shall become dear to the
good, good God, and replace Mary on this
earth again, and thus give joy to the Heart
of God.

Mary, Mother, come; reveal thyself to us,

that by knowing thee better, we may love thee better, and by loving thee be drawn by love to imitate thee.

---

It may be thought these readings for each day of the month of May are not sufficiently practical, but our desire has been to increase the love of God in the hearts of those who read, by showing how the love of God worked in the Heart of Mary. It is by this means we have hoped to increase the love of God in the hearts of our readers; and if there is real true love of God there will surely be a desire to fulfil His Will, by performing the duties of the state of life in which He has placed us. This is the only true criterion by which to know whether we have true love of God in our hearts, or have simply a sentimental feeling not worth the name of love. Then, dear Catholic readers, dear children of Mary, set to work to draw others to the love of God by your example. So let your light shine before men that they may see your good works, and glorify your Father who is in heaven. Sermons cannot do the work of good example. Priests may preach, sisters may instruct, books may be written, and all will

not have one iota of the effect which good
example will have, the example of good
living Catholics, of a body of people living in
unity, in love, "lives of love to God and
men," performing well the duties of their
state, not shirking, through indolence or
negligence, the work that has to be done in
this world, not making religion a cloak for
sloth. Ah, how much there is to regret in
good people, even apart from the bad Catholics, who are a disgrace to the Church, by
their breach of God's laws, by their breach of
all law, civil or divine; for besides these
there are so many good Catholics who would
be really sorry if they knew how much evil
they do by their supineness. It would, for
example, give one good gentleman too much
trouble to be a member of the School Board,
or of the Board of Guardians. Children
may be entered as Protestants in the work-
house, or in some other public institution,
because no one has taken the trouble to see
that they are entered as Catholics, etc., etc.
See what has happened in Catholic countries
when the Revolution has triumphed; see
how supine the good people of the country
were, and how active the wicked were, as
they always are. Could such outrages on
public honesty and decency, with reference to

the voting, have taken place if good' people had exerted themselves as they should have done? "Leave it to Providence," they will say, "leave all to God; we will pray." Yes, but God expects us to use natural means as well as supernatural. Why did He give us our faculties if we are not to use them? He loves to see His creatures exerting themselves on His behalf, diligently, earnestly, with all their mind and strength.

What a pity it is that we generally go to one extreme or the other. There are those who are too supine; and on the other hand, those who trust too much to their own activity, who do not confide in the providence of God sufficiently, perhaps not at all, and who seem bent on compassing their ends in spite of constituted authority, whether of the Church or of civil government; the Fenians, for example, the Socialists, the Nihilists, or by whatever other name they may be called, whose principles and mode of action cannot be too much abhorred.

We, on our part, must take the proper course, that which right reason and religion point out, uniting prayer with action, action with prayer, working whilst we may in all uprightness, leaving all to God when we have done our best. Working, in fact, according to the principle the saints have taught us, as though all the success depended on ourselves, whilst all the time we know that, work as we will, the success depends upon God alone. "God helps those who help themselves," is an old adage, which many might do well to meditate upon.

We hope not to offend any by this suggestion, and we trust it may be taken in good part, for our simple intention has been to impress upon those who read this little work in honour of the gentle, loving Mother of God, our own sweet Mother Mary, that if they feel their hearts burning with a new and unwonted love of Mary, they must put their love into action, by performing more perfectly the duties of their state of life, for such is the Will of God for them, and by such conduct alone can they please Him.

# THE HEART OF MARY.

Let us come apart from the many things of this world that engross our thoughts; let us withdraw our eyes from the visible objects by which we are surrounded, and let us cast them upon a wonderful work of God,—the Heart of Mary. In what does its excellence consist? First, it is immaculate; next, it is a Virgin Heart; lastly, it is the Heart of a Mother. That we may have other help, over and above what our own understanding and memory can give us, let us beg our Lord to grant us a special light, a gift from His Holy Spirit, to enable us worthily to appreciate this the most excellent of all His works, and to love it with a spark of the love with which He Himself loves the sweet Heart of His Mother.

If we use the natural means God gives us to understand, that by understanding we may be enabled to love and praise Him in His works, we may expect from Him a supernatural light to aid us; but for want of a proper use of the powers of the soul in those who have time, and opportunity, and likewise

good natural abilities, when they choose to
use them; because they neglect to use the
natural means which God has given them,
God refuses them the supernatural aid, without which studies, when directed to the works
of God, are of little use. Let us, then, use
the natural faculties our good God has bestowed upon us, and perhaps whilst doing so,
He, in His love, may put into our minds some
of His own thoughts.

What strikes us first, as we look upon the
Heart of Mary, is its purity. Its every im-
pulse and emotion was pure, and yet that
Heart was conceived in a fallen world, was
born on this sinful earth, a simply human
heart. There was no hypostatic union of
human nature with the divine to make it thus
immaculate, and yet that Heart never produced aught that savoured of this earth in its
present fallen state. Ah, let us but glance at
the multitude of unworthy thoughts and feelings conceived by our own sinful hearts, even
when they are not brought to birth, not wil-
fully indulged, and no sin is therefore committed, and comparing then the one pure
human Heart, that never conceived what was
in the least degree imperfect, with our own,
not only imperfect, not only selfish, but often
deliberately sinful heart, we shall discover

reason for thanking God that from the Heart
of one of His creatures worship has been
offered upon this earth, worship, adoration,
love such as angels offer, and greater than
angels offer. We rejoice that God has had,
does still have, and will ever have such deep,
pure adoration from one who is still but a
creature, not created in heaven, but on earth;
one who lived such a pure, beautiful, heavenly
life, though in such a sinful world; and as we
think of this we resolve that our hearts shall
harmonize with the Heart of that fair one, that
we will think and meditate upon the loves of
the Heart of Mary, that we too may love as
she did, and thus please the good God of love.
" Accipio te in mea omnia. Præbe mihi cor
tuum, O Maria."

This we must desire, to live with Mary's
Heart. Will you be wearied at my repeating
the same thing so often? It has a different
meaning from what you may suppose. It
leads to a very high perfection. It leads you
to desire, to love, to act, not from natural
inclination, even though such inclination be
good, but to live by, with, in Mary's Heart,
so that you desire, you love, you act in union
with it. There were various loves in the
Heart of Mary. There was her love for God
her Creator; there was her love for God her

Son; her love for us. All these various loves
in the Heart of Mary brought her various joys,
but likewise many sorrows. So we shall find
with ourselves, "there is no living in love without sorrow;" but still, if the sorrow makes us
a little less sinful, a little less selfish, shall we
not rejoice, shall we not be glad, shall we not
thank God with great gratitude, that He has
shown such goodness to us, by purifying us,
by making us more pleasing in His sight, by
making us in some little degree to resemble
that loving, gentle, sorrowing, suffering Heart
of our Mother, the fairest, the most beautiful
object in creation, after the Sacred Humanity
of our Lord, to the eyes of God?

Mother, sweet Mother, thou art called our
Lady of Pity; thy Heart was ever full of
tenderest love and pity. So great was thy
love on earth that thou wouldst willingly have
lived on here had God permitted it, if by
doing so thou couldst have saved the sinful
children of earth. So great is thy love in
heaven that thou wouldst leave it to save but
one of God's creatures from eternal ruin.
Little they are in the eyes of men; carelessly,
ah, worse! unkindly, cruelly, do we treat them,
but they are great to thee, they are great in
the sight of God. Thou couldst not do for us
on earth what thou canst do in heaven, or thou

wouldst willingly come from heaven to do it.
But live again in thy children, sweet Mother,
live on earth in thy own.  Renew in them thy
tender compassion, thy burning love, thy forgetfulness of self.  Would that we could taste
and feel within ourselves what thou didst feel.
But what was this love of Mary?  It was an
ardent desire of the possession of, and of union
with, the children of earth, because they are
the children of God, made to His likeness, and
redeemed by the Blood of her Son, with a persevering willingness to suffer all things rather
than that one should be lost.

And this is the love thou wouldst, sweet
Mother, that thy children should have.  It is
thy entreating prayer thou wouldst have them
offer, the prayer that never ceased in the midst
of thy daily occupations, the prayer of thy
Heart.  We do love thee, Mary our Mother.
Here in thy own home our prayer shall never
cease; though we may not be always watching
in choir as we would wish to be able to do,
still we will live as though our home was thy
Heart, as though we were living in thy great
Heart of love, constantly offering our *actions*
for the same intention as though we were
praying,—and indeed the action is a prayer,—
assisting in spirit at the Masses that are being
offered for the same intention.  Even in time

of recreation this can be done: it needs but an instant's thought to join in the Kyrie, Gloria, Offertory, Sanctus, Elevation, Communion, and so on. Union with Mary brings the power our Lady possessed of thinking of heavenly things whilst employed in the commonest things, the smallest every-day actions.

Let us, then, keep ever in the spirit of our Mother. Let us foster that spirit. If we feel it springing up within us, though it be but a beginning, let us tend it carefully. A feeling of devotion, of love, a maternal feeling, will often come into our minds. It is a grace from God. Let us, then, not neglect the grace. Let us make the little bud blossom. When we feel disinclined to do some action painful to nature, let us remember we have to make our bud blossom. When, mayhap, we wake in the morning unrefreshed, half rested, weary, when it needs a great effort to rise, let us remember our blossom that has to become fruit. Let us remember the grace God gave us, of feeling that we loved Him so much, of wishing to please Him all we could, and for that end desiring to become like our own dear Mother Mary. This remembrance will help us to overcome our weariness. Only by continued acts, acts contrary to nature, painful

to it, can we become like Mary. We have to
become what all Mary's own must be,—
mothers,—and that not in a half-and-half kind
of way. Oh, no. What can be worse than a
cold-hearted, neglectful mother? Certainly it
were better not to be one at all than to be a
bad one. No; we will be devoted, generous
mothers to all who need our care, whether for
their souls or bodies. God be praised, He is
good indeed; He will give us all the grace we
need, as much, I might almost say, as we
choose to take: and we want grace. We
need to have our hearts in union with Mary's
Heart. Young virgin hearts you have now,
my children, and you know not the change
that will be worked in them by God's power;
but this cannot be done without suffering.
The quiet placidity, the gentle wish to do
good to others, the sisterly love, is changed
into an intense burning love, an ardent zeal, a
consuming desire to save souls. There will
come to the most perfect among you a longing
to suffer, an efficacious determination to suffer.
When these graces come treasure them, value
them, nurture them. Remember that the
graces we possess may be lost, may wither and
die away, unless carefully tended and fostered.
We have thought of our dear Lord's suffering.
We have felt the longing rise within us to

participate in it. We have earnestly wished to be like Jesus, and yet when the suffering came, how little was it borne in a Christ-like, Mary-like spirit? And thus we lose a great grace and gift of God, which would have drawn us closer to Him, and strengthened our virtue, made it solid, given us power to work in the souls of others. God grant us this grace of graces, the grace to suffer well. It is through Mary our Mother we shall receive it, Mother of divine grace, sweet Mirror of patience, Mother of sorrow.

The Maternal Heart of Mary, the Heart of our Mother, the Mother-Heart of Mary, the Heart near which Jesus rested in peaceful repose for nine months, and the gentle beatings of which were sweeter music to Him than the hymns of angels! Ah, sweet Mother, we are the children of that Maternal Heart; we have bound ourselves to procure its honour, we are banded to promote its interests, we love it with an overwhelming love. How shall we honour it, how shall we show our love for the Heart our Mother? How shall we do what Jesus so loves us to do—honour the Heart of His Mother? "Honour the Heart of My Mother," our dear Lord seems to say to us. We have come, dear Jesus, to do so. How shall we

do it? We do love Thy Mother-Heart,—
our Mother-Heart. How shall we show our
love? By imitating it. Yes, that is what
Jesus wants; He longs to see His Mother
again living on earth in her children, as far
as may be. He wants to see children of
Mary, with virgin mother-hearts within
them; that is what He is asking from us
now. Mary is the Mother above all mothers,
Mary is the model of motherhood; and we
cannot be like our Mother Mary unless we
too have mothers' hearts. If we keep close
in her company, if we lean upon her and
trust her, if we ask her to show us the love of
her sweet Maternal Heart, we shall gradually
grow like it, we shall imbibe its spirit; such
a beautiful spirit it is, such a loveable one.
Little by little we shall feel it is growing up
within us: the change may be imperceptible
at first, but there will come by degrees a
new feeling, a maternal feeling, new to us,
superseding our old feeling of self-love, and
what is better than any feeling at all, in-
ducing us to do greater things for the good of
others. We have had perhaps a sister's love,
we may have had an apostolic love of souls,
we may have longed to do good to others,
and yet this love was quite a different thing
from the new love we find our Mother is

putting into our hearts, this mother-love for others; and this mother-love has such an intensity, is so much a passion, that our hearts seem different ones from what they were,—we hardly know them now. This is the perfection we children of the Maternal Heart of Mary are to aim at; it will bring such graces upon the world when Jesus can look down and see this Mother-love of Mary spread over the world in every country. The pleadings of a mother will be ever ascending before God, that beautiful unselfish cry of a true mother; we shall, hidden in our Mother's Heart, send up the pure incense of prayer from our unselfish hearts: a loving maternal feeling for those around will induce a constant cry for mercy for them, and mercy will come; God's mercy will be ever descending as the maternal prayer of Mary's Heart is sent from earth to heaven by Mary's children on earth; the hopeful, imploring, loving cry will be most pleasing to God, and His benediction will certainly come from heaven to earth upon those poor erring ones for whom it is thus implored, and a double benediction likewise for those who ask, and who plead as if for their own salvation, and who thus fulfil our dear Lord's command by loving others as He has loved them.

In the convent, in the world, wherever we may be, we should be ever resting on our Mother's breast, drinking in from it grace and life; grace to live as the Mother of Divine Grace lived, grace to live an unworldly, unselfish life, a life of love, pure maternal love, love as strong, nay, stronger than death.

Another quality of this prayer, which endears it to God, is that it is so hopeful. A mother never despairs when praying for her child, she could not live if she did. A mother ever hopes, she hopes on and on, even against all hope. The children of the Mother of holy hope imbibe her spirit, though at times their prayer is a prayer of anguish and grief, of bitter sorrow, when some soul that they are specially interested in, for which they feel in a certain sense responsible, seems obdurate, hardened, and the devil seems entire master of it; and then the Mother of sorrow lets this child, praying on her breast, taste a little, and indeed it is but a very little, of her own sorrow at the view of her lost children, and this child of Mary is pierced with the awful thought,—suppose this soul, for whom I pray, this soul which I so love, should finally be lost; then its spirit seems as it were, to hear the wail of agony from the Heart of Jesus, and it grieves still more

at the grief of its Lord, which it then realizes
to be immeasurable, to be beyond its knowledge. The thought arises, if I can suffer so
much from the dread of one I love being lost,
how must Jesus have suffered from the knowledge He had that many He loved would be
lost, so many, for He loved all, every human
being that would ever live. These thoughts
will often make Mary's children pray with an
agonizing earnestness, with a piteous pleading
most pleasing to God. In general, however,
and as a rule, cheerfully, (though, as we have
said, not always so, and not always hope-
fully,) will their cry of petition ascend to
God. Children of Mary, will you not imitate
your Mother? Would you not wish to be
like her? Will you be the dearest of
God's children on earth? Then be like His
favoured one; be like Mary. Look upon the
Virgin-Mother. Much as we love her title of
Blessed Virgin, is it to us like her title of
Mother? Do our hearts warm as we think of
her a pure Virgin as they do when we think
of our sweet, loving Mother Mary, our sorrowful Mother, our own Mother? We thank
God for thee, dear Mother; we thank the
good good God for giving thee to us. O God,
we love Thee for making Mary. We want to
be like her; give us grace to imitate her, to

purify our souls by penance, by contrition.
The purity of penance has its charms with
Thee, as well as the Immaculate Conception
of the ever Blessed Immaculate one.   Purity
is obtained by penance, and thus obtained is
the fruit of Jesus's Passion as well as Mary's
purity, which too, was the fruit of the Passion
of Jesus.   Let us strive for this purity of
penance first.   Let us go on striving and
straining every nerve to obtain this blessed-
ness of penance, this purity of a contrite
humble heart, for upon this foundation all
good securely rests.   Then we shall grow in
every grace; then can God give abundant
grace.   Then shall we be able to follow our
Mother so as to become like her, so as to be
most pleasing to our dear Lord, by being thus
like to His Blessed Mother.   All over the
earth we will reproduce Mary's holy life.
We will delight our dear Lord.   He shall,
we trust, look upon this world and see Mary-
like souls everywhere, mothers in heart and
soul.   Then will the words of the holy
prophet be in one sense fulfilled: "Give
praise, O thou barren that bearest not; sing
forth praise, and make a joyful noise: ....
for many are the children of the desolate,
more than of her that hath a husband, saith
the Lord."—*Isaias* liv. 1.

# THE
# LOVES WHICH REIGN

IN

# The Heart of Mary.

READINGS FOR EVERY DAY OF THE MONTH.

## FIRST DAY.

### The Love of the Heart of Mary for the Blessed Trinity.

Oh God, our God, Most Holy Trinity, we with our poor cold hearts find ourselves silent, stilled, struck speechless with the wonder, with the burning love, we find rising within us, as we raise our thoughts to that one great Object of our love, the beginning and the end of all things, the Ever-blessed Trinity. If we feel so awe-stricken as we contemplate this mystery; if we feel " that lips that the coal of the seraphim has not touched "* dare

* Father Faber.

scarcely utter words upon this great mystery, from the knowledge that no words could speak befittingly, could speak with sufficient reverence; if *our* hearts feel so much, what must the pure, beautiful, burning Heart of Mary have felt? Ah, it seems useless to attempt to fathom it. We know that our best endeavours, our greatest earnestness of search into that pure receptacle of love, the Heart of Mary, will not discover to us all we would wish to discover. But, sweet Mother, we will still strive to know all we can, and we will ever remember that our best thoughts are nevertheless far, far below the reality.

We will look upon the Immaculate Virgin pouring out her soul to the Ever-blessed Trinity in the beautiful psalms of David, that are to this day the appointed praise of the Church of God, and daily chanted in so many holy spots. To what can we compare the song of praise of Mary?

Have we ever listened to a little bird trilling its lay, gently, and then more boldly, till finally its little heart seems ready to burst with the energy with which it pours out its song? Its whole little being seems employed to sing the best, the most it can. We watch and listen with delight. How, then, did Mary's God listen to the song of praise her

Heart sent forth to Him? Ah, we must be near God to know. When hereafter we lie upon His bosom we shall know a little of the joy the prayer and praise of the Heart of Mary gave her Creator. Truly she followed the injunction of the apostle, "Singing and making melody in your hearts to the Lord, giving thanks always for all things." No creature of God, angel or saint, has ever rejoiced in God as Mary did. "We give Thee thanks for Thy great glory" has been the loving antiphon of saints, but none sang it as Mary did. Her God was happy, therefore was she happy. Her God was good, was all perfection, all peace, all joy, all holiness, all beauty, possessing all things within Himself; He could do all things; His power, as all else, was simply infinite, illimitable; His various attributes ineffable. Her God was Three Persons, all equally beautiful, great, and good. Her God was the Father, possessing, rejoicing in the Son. Her God was the Son, resting in "unruffled repose in the bosom of the Father." Her God was the Holy Spirit, proceeding from Father and Son, "the link of love of Father and Son." And these Three Persons of the Blessed Trinity were adored, and praised, and glorified, and loved by Mary as by none other of God's creatures; indeed,

Mary understood the mystery of the Blessed
Trinity as none other of God's children have
ever or will ever understand it. Thanks be
to the Most High. We are glad, O Mary,
that it is so ; we rejoice that thou didst love,
and dost love, the Ever-blessed and Adorable
Trinity as none others ever have or ever
will. So be it, sweet Mother. But still
give to thy children some little of thy spirit,
that they too may rejoice and find comfort
in their sorrow, from the great truth that
must give joy if rightly thought of,—the joy
of God, the joy of the Three Persons of the
Most Holy Trinity.

## SECOND DAY.

### The Love of the Heart of Mary for the Eternal Father.

You have received the spirit of adoption,
whereby we cry " Abba, Father!" Who can
say this as Mary said it ? to whom can it so
well apply ? Abba, Father ; ah, would that
we knew the joy of God as He bent attentive
ear to that cry from His fair daughter Mary.
Abba, Father ! it was sweet to the mouth of

Mary; she loved from a child to repeat it. It was indeed " honey-comb to the mouth, music to the ear, joy to the heart." Abba, Father! she heard it in after time, when she became a mother, spoken by other lips, the Human lips of Jesus, and it was sweeter still to her then. Is it sweet thus to us? do we say it as Jesus and Mary said it?

Our Father, Who art in Heaven. Do we linger over the words with the love and delight, with the hope and joy, with the sweet familiarity and reverence which the children of God should have for that great good Father, from Whom " all paternity is named"? "Father of my Lord Jesus Christ," spoke one of the spouses of Jesus; but yet she said it not as Mary said it. Oh, with what wondrous transport Mary spoke to her Father in heaven, the God Who had created her, Who had created her Immaculate; but still more did that Heart of Mary swell and exult, as she called upon the Eternal Father, on the Father of the Son of Love, the Father of the Son of Man, her Jesus.

Mary, sweet Mother, make thy children to love their Father in heaven; obtain for the brethren of Jesus to love the Father of Jesus, fill their hearts with the love, reve-

2

rence, confidence that should possess them; and thus will they glorify that good Father, Whose love created them, Whose love preserves them, pardons them, promises heaven to them, delights in declaring and proclaiming blessed those who on earth looked to Him their Father in heaven, who viewed Him ever as a Father, who prayed to Him as such, who trusted, revered, reverenced Him, and spread His love. " Holy Father, Thou hast hidden these. things from the wise and prudent, and hast revealed them to little ones;" to the little Virgin of Nazareth. Thou madest Thyself known; she rested in Thy sweet Fatherly embrace from the instant Thou didst bring her into existence; she never withdrew as we have done; she lived in Thy love.   Good, gentle Father, make us to live in it likewise, and make us so to pursue our way brightened by the lamp of Thy Fatherly love, trusting to it so confidently, that Thou mayest hereafter reward the hope within us by the Eternal bright Vision and enjoyment of Thyself in eternity.  May it be so, sweet Mother; do thou be our aid, our hope; give us some of thy love for the Eternal Father; the love with which thou didst love Him was, in some little measure, like the love with which He is loved by the Eternal Word, the

Son of His love; imprint Their love, dear Mother, in the hearts of thy children.

---

## THIRD DAY.

### The Love of the Heart of Mary for the Eternal Word.

Mary's love for the Son of God, the Second Person of the Blessed Trinity! We have said that Mary's love for the Eternal Father was not merely the love of a child of earth for its Father in heaven: but likewise a love in some sort similar to the love of the Eternal Word for the Father. There was a certain similarity, though not in degree, for in that respect there can be no likeness between the finite and the Infinite; so likewise, besides the adoration, the adoring love of the pure creature for the Word of God, by Whom all things were made, there was likewise a love, similar in some way, a distant counterpart, as it were, to the love of the Eternal Father for His Eternal Word.

Those who truly love God will understand this. If, however, you have not yet that love of God in your heart that you would wish to

have, love Mary, and it will sooner or later
come.  We are told to love God with our
whole hearts, our whole soul, with our whole
strength, that is, with our whole being.  We
may desire affective love if we would always
make it effective, and if we want to love God
in order to please God, and not that we may
please ourselves, which is an important point
worth considering and examining ourselves
upon.  If we would love God unselfishly we
must love Him as Mary loved Him.  We are
considering Mary's love for the Eternal Word ;
we are diving into the recesses of her sweet
Heart to discover all its loves.  It is like the
looming of some beautiful sanctuary of God,
where the very walls are consecrated and set
apart for God's service, and seem to echo and
re-echo, God ! love of God !  Silent, solemn,
yet simple in its solemnity is this sweet
Heart, now we want to feel its love for the
Son of God.  Such a wondrous love of the
possession of the Word of God was in the
Virgin Heart of Mary, such an intense longing,
which she knew not would be satisfied as it
afterwards was.  But so it is.  God so often
makes us intensely desire what He intends
finally to grant us.  Half the good works in
this world are thus accomplished.  The very
desire, if not an idle one, God accepts as a

prayer, and if so with us and our poor though earnest desires, how much more so with Mary? Mary sighed after the Son of God with an intense longing, implanted in her by the Father Himself, and how far, far beyond her expectation was her desire granted her. She truly possessed her God as none other ever has or ever shall.

Oh, beautiful one of God, so like Himself, so beautiful, so wonderful, in that thou art still, though so lovely, a simple creature of earth. Help us to possess and love Him too. Show us how to possess Him in this world as well as in the next, for many think not of this. We may, we should, possess our God here as well as hereafter. Mary will make you understand this great truth, which it is not given to all to understand, but the truly meek and humble of heart will realize it. Mary will illuminate your mind, she will open your understanding, she will enlighten you her true children. Sweet Mother, we are grateful that thou hast drawn us to thee, for now we begin to know our God as we never before knew Him. Abiding with thee, and enlightened by thee, Mary, our most dear Mother, we look upon our God, we see the Eternal Word locked in the embrace of the Everlasting Father; we look and love. O God, how wonderful Thou

art. We would that all could know Thee as
we now know Thee, as Mary shows Thee to
us. What else is to be desired, lived for,
loved, but our God, our own God, the just,
the generous, the beautiful? How great
must be the Father's love for us sinners. He
gave the Son of His love to die for us. How
the Son must love us, since He came on earth
from the bosom of His Father to dwell with
us. Yes, He came; "His delights are to be
with the children of men." Mother, may we
open our hearts to receive the Eternal Word
as thou didst. May we keep Him ever with
us, and never oblige Him to leave us. Amen.
Amen.

-----

# FOURTH DAY.

## The Love of the Heart of Mary for the Holy Ghost.

Mary, spouse of the Holy Ghost, bring us
light from His inaccessible throne. Gabriel
brought thee a marvellous message, sweet
Mother. "The Holy Ghost shall come upon
thee, and the power of the Most High shall
overshadow thee."

What was that wonderful overshadowing of
the Holy Spirit of God? Mary, we are diving
deeper into mysteries. We seem to fear
lest we may be attempting to know what God
has not intended we should know, since so little
is revealed. What passed in that wondrous
communion of Mary with the Holy Ghost
none but herself knoweth. The little Virgin of
Nazareth was encompassed with God's Spirit,
" overshadowed," and an ineffable communion
took place, flooding the soul of Mary with a
new joy, lifting her into regions of light and
love hitherto unexplored by her, opening her
Heart in a most mysterious manner, her
life absorbed as it were in God's life, the Holy
Spirit giving her new life, Mary yielding to
the sweet influence of the Spirit of God, God's
Spirit working in her without let or hindrance,
or disturbance, not meeting with the slightest
opposition in this wonderful creature of God
to the marvellously ineffable operations of
grace. Mary became the spouse of the Holy
Ghost and the Mother of God. These simple
words are enough ; human language can do no
more. But what concerns us to know is, that
the Holy Ghost still works and loves to work
by her. He formed Jesus by means of Mary,
and to this day He forms all the elect by means
of Mary. He formed His master-piece, the

God-Man, the Head of the elect, by Mary, and
will continue to form the members of that
Head by the same sweet means, His spouse
Mary. And well does Mary co-operate with
Him. Entirely possessed by God's Spirit,
she lives by that Spirit; she is ever working
in the souls of men by bringing the Holy
Ghost to breathe the breath of life into wither-
ing souls, animating her children too to bring
all they can to the influence of that sweet
Spirit of God. The more we love God's Spirit
ourselves, the more we shall make others love
it too, and the more good we shall do.

Let us then daily, hourly, beg our Mother
to make us know the Third Person of the
Blessed Trinity better, that we may have
light to understand better what is indeed
difficult to be understood, for we have nothing
analogous to it in creation; there are no
comparisons or resemblances which will help
us. When we study the spirit of a Saint, in
whom the Holy Ghost has made His dwelling, we come to know something of his interior thoughts, feelings, etc.; but still this
does not reveal to us the secret and mysterious working of the Holy Spirit of God, and
much less can we fathom or explain the ineffable operations of the Holy Ghost in Mary
the Mother of God. However, though we

cannot write or speak about this Adorable
Mystery, if we keep close to our Mother we
shall think beautiful thoughts, we shall have
holy, truthful ideas, far though they may be
below the reality; we shall have conceptions
of divine truths, though we may not be able
to give expression to them in words, yet they
will leave their impress upon the mind, they
will do the work God intends they should;
the Holy Spirit will work in us, forming us
into noble children of God, and He will do it
most admirably by means of Mary, and by
our devout meditation on the mysteries of
Mary. Ah, sweet Mother, thou wert made
a mother by the working of the Holy Ghost;
thou lovest that Holy Spirit Who possessed
thee in all thy ways with a supereminent
love, and this love we thy children would
wish to share with thee. Thou lovest thy
Spouse, the Holy Ghost, Who made thy
Virgin Heart a mother's heart. Teach thy
children to love Him too, for beautiful will
the souls become that are placed in the care
and keeping of the Holy Ghost by the hands
of Mary. Mother, plead for us. Pointing to
thy Heart, which the Holy Ghost hath made
a Mother's heart, intercede with that sweet
Spirit for thy numberless children, who now,
banded round that Heart, desire but to live in

union with it, who so love it, to whom it is as
an anchor of safety, a port of refuge, a beacon
of light in the dark storms of life, a fair
sanctuary of safety, our happy home, we
trust, with God for all eternity.

Mary, Spouse of the Holy Ghost, pray for
us!

---

## FIFTH DAY.

### The Love of the Heart of Mary for the Precious Blood.

The Precious Blood, the beautiful stream
of Life, rising first in the fair fount of Mary's
Heart, becoming *Precious* in the Heart of
Jesus, flowing on from thence to the souls of
men, making them likewise precious in their
degree in the sight of God, with the Infinite
purity, the brightness of that Precious Blood
of Jesus upon them.   How must Mary have
loved the Precious Blood?   Only those who
have an ardent burning love for the Precious
Blood themselves, can enter in some slight
degree into Mary's feelings, and understand
something, little though it be, of her love.
We look upon the priest at Mass with holy
envy, as he raises the chalice containing the

Blood of Jesus. That wondrously privileged man may look to his heart's content upon the lovely Blood of his Lord; he is indeed happy; he is a favoured being, but not so as Mary was. She raised that Precious Blood in Its living Chalice in the Infant Heart of Jesus; she lifted It to the Most High; she pressed It to her breast as the greatest Treasure this world had seen; she watched It in the translucent veins of that divine, that most lovely Child, and she loved It,—how she loved It! Mother, make thy children love It too, and they will spread Its glory; they will not cease their endeavours, that there may not be a soul on earth they have not brought to be cleansed, purified, brightened by that most Precious Blood.

We will also honour the Precious Blood in our own souls. We will love the sacraments, the channels of the Precious Blood to us. We will honour the Precious Blood ever present in our tabernacles. We will specially honour the Precious Blood when we receive it in Holy Communion. We will make reparation to it, we will raise it in reparation to the Most High, for our own sins and the sins of a sinful world. We will press in spirit loving kisses on the price of our redemption, we will press it to our hearts with Mary. We at least, Mary's children, will love Thy Precious Blood, dear Jesus. We will draw all whom we can influence to love and honour that sweet Blood, the Blood shed with so great love to save the souls of men. Mary loved the Blood that would give her children, she loved the Blood that would make her children the children of God, which would change the children of earth and of darkness into children of light and heaven. She loved the Blood that had purchased her own Immaculate Conception; she loved the Blood that had formed and cemented the Church; she loved the Blood that enabled her, that enabled all the creatures of this earth, to worship with befitting worship the God of all, the Creator of all; she loved the Blood by which we may offer to God adoration, praise, thanksgiving, greater than the cherubim and seraphim could of themselves offer in countless ages. Yes, the Blood of the Heart of Jesus was the love of the Heart of Mary. It was her constant joy, her perpetual delight, her precious treasure, her pure praise, her brightest beam of sunshine in this world. It is now her blessed content in the peaceful world above, in her everlasting rest in the bosom of the God who, having been all in all to her in this life, is all in all to her in the true life, the life we hope to enjoy with her one day in heaven.

" O God, whose goodness is infinite, and whose property it is always to have mercy and to spare, the children of a sinful world seek Thy mercy through the Heart of Thy Mother. In the sweet Heart of Thy Mother Mary they seek refuge. May the pleading of that Heart be heard by Thee. May the Precious Blood that Heart furnished, here present upon Thy altar, appease Thy justice, rightly irritated by the sins of men. May Thy Holy Spirit move upon the troubled waters of this fallen world, and let there be light, the light of Thy mercy, O God, Most Holy Trinity, whose mercy is magnificent, and will shine by Mary for ever and ever. Amen.

" Precious Blood of my God, my Jesus, Saviour of mankind, prostrate in lowliest adoration we worship Thee, and make solemn reparation for the outrages that have been and now are offered Thee on this earth. Blood of the Lamb slain from the foundation of the world, delight of the Father, draw His mercy yet more. Jesus, in union with the holy Angels adoring the Precious Blood Thou didst shed in Thy Passion, we adore.

" Jesus, we sinful creatures, who caused the insults offered to Thy Precious Blood during

Thy painful Passion, beg forgiveness, and adoring, offer reparation. Jesus, in union with the Mother-Heart that adored and grieved, and was pierced with sorrow at the outrages offered to the Precious Blood that Heart had furnished, Mary's children, in union with their Mother, offer reparation, whilst they honour the Heart of Thy Mother as Thou desirest. Father, thus through the Blood of Thy beloved Son Jesus we invoke Thy Holy Spirit, whilst we offer reparation due to the Blood that saved Thy saints now reigning with Thee in heaven, that we hope may save Thy children still on earth. For this Thy great mercy we will praise Thee, through Him whose Blood is now raised at Thy right hand, and adored for ever and ever. Amen."

## SIXTH DAY.

### The Love of the Heart of Mary for the Sacred Heart.

Who was the first lover and adorer of the Sacred Heart? Mary. We do not always recollect that. We honour and venerate greatly the saint who promoted the devotion to the

Sacred Heart, (she was one of Mary's own,) and we do rightly. But let us ever recollect that Mary was the first, as she was above all comparison the greatest lover of the Heart of Jesus. Sweet devotion of the Immaculate Mother to the Heart of the Infant Jesus! Whilst Mary bore it within her she perpetually offered the Heart of her Son, with its treasure of Precious Blood, to the Eternal Father, as continual adoration. With what content, with what extatic joy, did Mary thus worship the Ever-blessed Trinity! When she had sung the praises of God in the temple, when her whole being, burning with love, had poured itself out a living sacrifice of pure love, holy, pleasing to God, yet longed she to offer more; and now she can do so, and with unspeakable content she does do so.

Jesus lies in His chosen tabernacle in Mary, peaceful, silent as He lies in the tabernacle on the altar. Before Him burns a perpetual lamp, fragrant flowers are ever before Him, and incense unceasingly offered. The Heart of Mary it is that furnishes this worship. The pure flame of love sent forth from her Heart of love pleased, delighted the Heart of Jesus; the beautiful flowers ever growing in Mary, " the garden of the new paradise," were virtues and graces that other creatures of God have never possessed as Mary did; and the prayer of her Heart was the incense that indeed is pleasing to God. Thus was Mary happy in being able to offer what she knew rendered Jesus such unspeakable joy. He, whose delight is to be with the children of men, superabounded with delight in being with Mary.

But Mary remained not in quiet communion with Jesus, in the enjoyment of her own happiness in possessing Him. Oh no; she had a duty to perform, which she loved to perform. She had to do, through Jesus, with Jesus, and for Jesus,—who was now before birth in complete dependence upon her, living by her breath,—what He had come to do, to offer to the Eternal Father the adoration and thanksgiving human nature never yet had befittingly offered; to offer atonement for the sins committed on this sinful earth; to thank the Ever-blessed Trinity for all the gifts bestowed upon mankind; and to implore for poor human nature a restoration to its original dignity. None felt so much as Mary did the degradation of mankind since the fall. None grieved so over it, as she thought how very beautiful God had made His creatures, and how terribly they had spoiled His work. Her own Immaculate Conception made her feel it as none other could. Therefore had she mourned nights and days as she saw the human race, whom God had made so great, so terribly fallen; and from this Mary's children must learn a lesson. They too must grieve and mourn, after the example of their Mother. "Blessed are they that mourn, for they shall be comforted." God shows us plainly how dear this mourning is to Him, how acceptable, by His promise to spare Sodom, if ten just could be found who mourned for the sins of that wicked city, but they were not found. But in the day when God's justice seeks to show forth and avenge itself upon a world teeming with sin, may it be stayed, may the just ones be found to stem the just anger of an all-holy God. In that day may there be those of Mary's own after her own Heart, whom she may show to the Almighty, grieving and mourning at His goodness so greatly outraged. Ah, for the sake of His elect may God shorten the day of His anger.

Mary possessed the Sacred Heart: she was its Mother; she had a right over it. Did she let her power, then, lie dormant? No, indeed no. A fervent priest, we know, will not omit, without the greatest necessity, the power he has to do good by offering the Holy Sacrifice; but no priest ever possessed the fervour of Mary, however saintly he may have been. Mary therefore performed, with ever-increasing fervour and love, the office, we might almost say, of priest, since she called God from heaven by her word, and then offered the Son to the Eternal Father in deepest adoration as the supreme act of worship due to Him. No priest ever offered the Precious Blood with the dispositions with which Mary offered it in the golden chalice of the Sacred Heart.

Mother, thou seemest to be all things in one; perfect creature and adorer of thy Creator, and yet Mother of the Son of God, and, though a Mother, a pure Immaculate Virgin. Now we see thee as priest.

What are Mary's own to learn from this thought of Mary? That they must imitate her. But how? Keep Jesus with you. He will willingly stay. " He that eateth My Flesh, and drinketh My Blood, abideth in Me and I in him." Jesus will dwell with you. He desires to do so. " I seek a pure heart, and there is the place of My abode." Why not, then, strive to keep Him? When He dwells in a soul, that soul does good wherever she goes, insensibly to herself perhaps, but so it will be. Her words will have weight, her actions will fructify and produce good she had

not intended, because she did not think of it.
She may speak or write, and the words spoken
or written will be more the words of God than
her own, and the words of God are works,
especially to docile souls. To such this soul
possessing Jesus will have great power. Let
that soul speak to a good child, for instance,
telling it to pray for her, and that child will
feel urged in a wonderful manner to pray. A
simple soul once thought how happy it must
be to be a priest, to be able to bless and do
good wherever it went; but those who are not
priests may bless and do good wherever they
go if they carry Jesus with them.

He thirsts for souls imbued with the spirit
of Mary, Mary-like souls whom He can draw
to Himself with ineffable delight, to whom He
can make Himself known as He so desires to
do, with whom He can repose in peace, for
there will be nought to ruffle and disturb His
repose. " The Lord loveth the gates of Sion
more than all the tabernacles of Jacob." He
will love to be on earth with Mary again in
her children far more than in the tabernacles
of our churches, where He is often so neglected, so coldly treated.

# SEVENTH DAY.

## The Love of the Heart of our Lady for the Blessed Sacrament.

Sweet Mother, when we think of thy love for the Blessed Sacrament, we seem incapable of aught but to kneel, silently contemplating this ineffable mystery itself, and to offer it thy love.

Mary and the Blessed Sacrament! Our Lady is Mother of the Blessed Sacrament. No creature of God, not even the angels, understands this incomprehensible mystery as Mary does. Let us, bowing down in lowly adoration before our God, whose love has induced Him to work this great, grand work of wisdom, power, and love, ask humbly our Mother to feed us with some of her love for this adorable mystery of faith.

Years rolled on after the Ascension of our Lord, and these years were filled by Mary with acts of love for her Incarnate God, acts of love from a mere creature such as this world had never witnessed, and never will again. The ages roll on above, and find Mary still entranced with wondering love at the contemplation of the life of delight which Jesus leads with the children of men, the Word of God dwelling on earth. Oh, that sacramental life of Jesus. The saints were ever drawn to this sweet sacrament of love. They learned wonderful things from their hidden Lover in the tabernacle, but they never knew what they now know as they view the Blessed Sacrament from their home in the bosom of God. How they wish that we on earth could realize better this mystery of faith, how they wish that the one great thought of our hearts should be "God on earth;" the one great desire that He should be loved and honoured. Yes, the same God on earth, the very same God who is the eternal delight and joy of heaven. We believe this, but with what a cold dead faith do the majority of Christians show their belief. Those who live by Mary's Heart, who live in its loves, they do feel some little of her love for Jesus in the Blessed Sacrament, and it assuages all their pains. " Jesus, my life, my love, sweet Jesus, good Jesus, come to me when I cannot come to Thee," cries the sick one from her bed of pain ; and He comes and strengthens her to suffer more for love of Him. " Jesus, sweet Jesus, compassionate Lord," cries the mourner, as she flings herself on her knees at

the altar rails, and tells her tale of grief; and
she comes away soothed, calmed, comforted.
" Merciful Jesus, have mercy on me, for I
have sinned," murmurs the penitent in the
silent church; and He pardons her.  " My
God and my all," speaks the heart of the child
of Mary, " I give Thee myself, soul and body.
Accept me as Thine own, make me Thy
spouse ;" and Jesus imprints a kiss of love
upon her soul that binds her to Him alone.
" My Lord and Master," whispers the youth,
" make me to labour for Thee and Thine ; I
will guard and feed Thy sheep;" and Jesus
leads him within the rails to the altar, there
to pronounce the mystic words that shall bring
the Lord of life into the hands of His priest,
who shall dispense Him as the food and life of
the souls of the sheep entrusted to him by his
Lord and Master.   " My Love, my only
Love, my most Beloved," cries the saint; and
Jesus dwells in the heart of the saint, whose
motto is, " God alone."   " Jesus, Lord, dear
Jesus," lisps the little child; and Jesus blesses
it, and loves the heart of that little one with
a love we none of us know.

Ah, dear Lord, whose delight is to be with
the children of men, Thou leadest a life Thou
lovest amongst us, and we love to think of
Thy joys; but there is another life Thou

leadest, and for which we would fain make reparation, a life in which we see Thee treated with coldness, neglect, even with hatred, even with insults. Oh Jesus, we cannot bear to think of it, and yet we know it is true, too true, and it makes us sad to think it should be so. But the children of Mary's Heart will love Thee hidden in the Blessed Sacrament; they will worship Thee; they will visit Thee where Thou remainest so hidden and so sweet; they will visit Thee in spirit when they cannot visit Thee in person; they will ask their guardian angels to carry messages of love to Thee; they will live for love of Thee, their sacramental God.

They will bring to Thee hearts somewhat like Thy Mother's, striving to love Thee as her Heart loves Thee, striving to love others as her Heart loves them, watching with Thee, keeping Thee company, O most patient Jesus, most forbearing Lord. We will grow more and more enamoured of our silent Lover, as we daily increase our visits to Him, and in the still church pour out our whole souls before the loving Heart that in the tabernacle beats day and night with burning love for each single soul amongst the sons of men, the children of earth, who are so callous and cold to

Him, and whom, nevertheless, He still so loves.

Mary, my Mother, take me thy child by the hand, and lead me to Jesus in the Blessed Sacrament. Speak to me of Him, and tell me what I shall say and do to please Him. Under cover of our Mother's mantle we approach. "My child," she seems to say, "bow down, Jesus is here, the Son of God, the Second Person of the Blessed Trinity, the Word made Flesh for love of men. Jesus is here, true God and true Man, the Sacred Heart, the very emblems of which all children of the Church so love. That very Sacred Heart is here within the tabernacle, beating, burning with love for thee. The Precious Blood, the very Blood that trickled in great drops from the hands and feet of Jesus, the very Blood that stained the sod of Calvary, is here. Prostrate and adore, prostrate and make reparation to the Precious Price of thy redemption. Still more, my child, the Blessed Trinity itself is here, Father, Son, and Holy Ghost." Oh Mother, speak no more, but worship thou for me. My God, the Great, the Mighty, the Most High, the Beautiful, the bright Light of lights, the God who is, who alone is, is here, and His court of angels are adoring Him. My Mother, now indeed thy child feels, in the presence of her God, how little worthy of the Almighty God is the highest worship that creatures can offer. But Jesus is here to offer worship in His Sacred Human Nature to the Blessed Trinity for poor mankind, and we may rejoice that human nature does offer worship befitting the Most High.

Thou art living in this world, sweet Jesus, and offering adoration, praise, thanksgiving, for us, and we thank Thee, we love Thee, for that Thou hast paid our debt to our God. " Look down, O Lord, from on high, from Thy dwelling-place, and behold the sacred Victim which our great High Priest, Thy Holy Child, our Lord Jesus, offers Thee for His brethren," for Mary's children. "Behold, the Blood of Jesus cries to Thee," and worships Thee for us, loves, adores Thy Divine Majesty, satisfies Thy divine justice, and makes Thee still bless this earth, and pronounce it good and pleasing in Thy sight as Thou from Thy heavenly throne lookest down upon it. May Mary's lilies float upon the waters of the Precious Blood, and may it, flowing throughout the world with those precious flowers, beautify the earth. May the Holy Spirit, moving upon the face of the troubled waters of this dark and stormy sea of life, bring calm

3

and joy and peace to the world, that joy and peace which spring from faith in the adorable mystery of the holy Sacrament of the Altar.

> "But peaceful was the night
>   Whereon the Prince of Light
>     His reign of peace upon the earth began.
>   The winds with wonder whist,
>   Smoothly the waters kiss'd,
>     Whispering new joys to the wild ocean,
>   Who now hath quite forgot to rave,
>   While birds of calm sit brooding on the charmed
>     wave."
>
>                                        MILTON.

## EIGHTH DAY.

### The Love of the Heart of our Lady for the Blessed Sacrament.—Continued.

The love of our Lady for the Blessed Sacrament. She has set us an example in this, as in all else. The Blessed Sacrament was indeed all in all to her. When Jesus left this world, and took away the visible presence of His sweet Human Body from us, Mary turned to His invisible presence in the Blessed Sacrament, pouring out her whole Heart to Him in adoration and love. And this is what we

must do. We must really live with the
thought ever in our minds, that our God is
living in this world with us. We must run to
visit Him with lively faith. We must turn
to the church where He dwells, and visit Him
in spirit, if we cannot actually visit Him in
person.

Do we sufficiently value our Lord's presence
with us? If we wake in the night, is our first
thought of Him? Do our thoughts constantly
turn to Him in the day? Ah indeed, He
should never be out of our thoughts. He has
put Himself in our hands. He, our dear Lord,
is dependent upon us. Do we pay Him
court? Do we honour Him as we should?
Jesus, dear Jesus. How good, how very good
He is. He is ours, we are His. We must
visit Him as Mary did, as she would if now on
earth. We are to do what she would have us
do, we are to be in her place in this world.
To make our visits pleasing to Him we must
each of us strive more and more for some of
Mary's virtues. If we each endeavoured to
obtain one, and gradually became more perfect
in it; if in each of our hearts Jesus saw there
something resembling what was in His dear
Mother's Heart, how His Sacred Heart would
be gladdened when we come to visit Him: and
to give joy to Jesus, to do one little thing in

the day to please Him, how earnest and how glad we should be. What good do we do when we are seeking to please ourselves? At all events, we do not succeed. After a conversation, for instance, where we have been selfish; after an action mixed up with vain-glory; after a time devoted to some trivial matter, not through obedience, which makes trivial matters great, but from little selfish motives of self-indulgence; what a void there is in our souls. Whereas, when we have unselfishly given up ourselves, made a sacrifice cheerfully, how light-hearted we are, how happy. Why is this? Besides the testimony of a good conscience, we may believe that our guardian angel is pouring joy into us. He is full of joy himself whenever he sees a little less of self in us, and he makes us partakers of his joy. He wants so to see us like Jesus, he so desires to see us like his King and Lord. Why do we not think more of the good powerful friend, the brother, the protector, we have constantly by our side? Why do we not more constantly have recourse to him?

Let us go into the presence of our dear Lord, and there kneeling and adoring, thank Him for His great love and condescension to us. We have Him, He is all our own, He is here for us. How can we ever repay Him?

What can we do to show our love ?   Ah, we
will strive to be humble if we have but little
virtue.   Let us humble ourselves on account
of this, and come into our dear Lord's presence
to offer Him a contrite, humble heart, and
then let us make a spiritual communion, let
us draw Him close to us.   He longs to begin
on earth that union for which He made us,
which will be consummated in heaven.   It
seems as though it were too long for Him to
await our death.   Let us but prepare a place
for Him in our hearts, and He will come and
abide there, for so He promises, " He that
eateth My Flesh and drinketh My Blood
abideth in Me and I in him."   " If any man
love Me, My Father will love him, and We
will come to him, and make Our abode with
him."   Yes, Jesus has already made His
abode with us; we have Him on our altars.
We should ever be sending our thoughts
thither, even when absent from Him.   But
the happiest souls will so prepare an altar for
Him within themselves that their hearts will
be a tabernacle well pleasing to Him.   A far
more pleasing abode indeed is the human
heart to Jesus than the tabernacle of our
altars.   Those are happy souls who ever keep
Jesus with them, who so live that He can and
does come close to them, taking His delight

in them, and filling them with the peace and
joy that must ever accompany His holy
presence. How we forget our dear Lord,
how weak our faith is, how little we realize
His presence.

Our Creator, our God is here, the Blessed
Trinity, Father, Son, and Holy Spirit. The
angels are surrounding God's throne on earth.
We poor human beings should bow ourselves
humbly, contritely, acknowledging our unworthiness to be in His holy presence, and then
offer to the Blessed Trinity, offer to our good
God His own great glory, wish we could worship Him befittingly, wish that we poor human
beings could adore Him as He deserves to be
adored, and then look lovingly to our dear
Lord in the Blessed Sacrament, and offer
the adoration which the Sacred Heart is ever
offering for us, not indeed forgetting the glories
of our God in His glorious heaven, the beatific
vision, the beautiful face of the unspeak-
ably lovely God, who has made us to see and
enjoy Him for ever: for we must ever remember the glorious vision we hope to see
in heaven, the blissful presence we hope to
enjoy, while we bow down before the Sacred
Humanity of our dear Lord, the presence
which is now so much nearer and dearer to
us, the Blessed Sacrament of the Altar, which

on earth it is our happiness and privilege to
possess.   Ah Jesus, look upon us unworthy,
as we bend low before Thy divine presence,
humbled, contrite.   Mary, cover thy children
with thy maternal mantle of Mother-love, and
bless us.   If at this moment Jesus stood before us, as He did after His resurrection before
His dear Mother and His disciples, what would
be our feelings, what should we say?   There
would be a passing thought of our own utter
unworthiness; there would be a thought of our
sins, awakening within us a purifying act of
contrition, and then the thought of ourselves
would pass away in our thought of Him.   Our
hearts would say, "Jesus, most blessed, most
beautiful; Jesus radiant, glorious; Jesus, my
love, my life;" and we should raise our eyes to
His sacred countenance.   We can do so in
spirit now.   Our Lord is very near to us; we
are never out of His presence.   We should
therefore do all our acts as though we saw
Him present.   All our actions should be
performed as the priest does his when he
is following the rubrics of the Church carefully, methodically, not dilatorily, almost
swiftly, and yet with such attention and in so
orderly a manner.   All is put in its place, the
chalice, veil, the paten, and so on.   We have
all watched the priest at such times, and

noticed his carefulness. What should we think of one who left the chalice veil on one part of the altar, the paten on another, who was slovenly, disorderly, careless, whilst offering the Adorable Sacrifice of the Altar? Would it not make us shudder? Now the life of every Christian, especially of Mary's own, should be a sacrifice: every act should be done in this spirit. "Present your bodies a living sacrifice, holy, pleasing to God." We are offered, we are not our own. Our works, our thoughts, ourselves, our whole beings, are His. Therefore we will not "make rapine in the holocaust." Our works shall be done for our Lord. He is watching us. He is being offered in sacrifice. We are offering Him hour by hour in our works. We are offering His Precious Blood; whilst we are performing our works with the utmost fidelity we are offering the dear Blood of our Lord, and our thought of Him helps us to perform them in the proper spirit. Our spirit of prayer makes us so work as that it may be evident to those around us that we are working in His dear presence, and for Him whom we have promised to live for, to work for, to love alone.

Mary, sweet Mother, we are thy property. We know when we are visiting Jesus, when we are receiving Him in holy communion, when we are keeping Him in our hearts, that we are doing what you would have us do; therefore we will live with the thought that we have our God on earth with us. All our works shall be performed well, that we may present them as flowers, fair flowers of earth indeed, but still exhaling something of the fragrance of paradise, that we have gathered to offer to our God on our next visit to Him. He shall not be neglected as He has been heretofore; we will visit Him for our own sakes and for the love we bear Him, and we will visit Him too that we may make reparation for those who do not visit Him, and wherever we are, we who are Mary's own, in whatever place we may be, there Jesus shall be honoured, there He shall be adored and loved. Dear God, sweet Lord, who should indeed have love, since He gave His own life for love.

# NINTH DAY.

## The Love of the Heart of Mary for St. Michael.

> " O, who is that golden spirit
> So intently gazing there?
> O look, look upon his beauty,
> E'en in heaven how passing fair!
> God Himself, O grand Archangel,
> Deems thee bright beyond compare."

It is Michael the Archangel, the first creature who ever saw God, the prince and leader
of all the angels, the prince of all the heavenly
host, the head of the army that fought for God,
who raised the grand cry " Who is like unto
God ?" the cry that has come from heaven to
earth, the cry that all who love God love,
the cry that teaches us the character of the
beautiful prince of the angels, and therefore
the character of all the angels. All good
Christians love and venerate St. Michael; and
how then does the Mother of Christians, how
does Mary love St. Michael? Let us try and
get a glimpse of heaven. There is our Mother,
the angels' queen. Those bright spirits are
clustered round her; they are gazing upon

the spotless one; they look as though they
are anxious, as indeed they are, to perform
some service for her, to carry some message
to some favoured child; and there is one
more beautiful than all, there is one more
grand, more great, more gracious, who towers
above all the angelic host, more bright, more
glorious still. That one is Michael, Mary's
special messenger, Mary's most beloved of all
the angels; Michael, who watches with such
loving care Mary's Son Jesus in the Blessed
Sacrament; Michael, who seems to guard
Mary too; her ambassador on earth, her
champion, her protector, though she needs no
protector now, but having once held that
office, as we may piously believe, when she
lived on earth, he now enjoys the honoured
title by a special privilege, for the honour God
has once bestowed is not withdrawn. But be
this so or not, there is the glorious archangel
enthroned, and by a special prerogative he
seems to be Mary's Michael. It may be
that, as some hold, the rebel angels would not
acknowledge Mary, they would not bow to a
creature of earth, a woman who should be
higher than themselves, and that Michael
stood up then as Mary's champion, and proclaimed her blessed above all creatures, and
there and then acknowledged her his queen,

and thus Mary now graciously acknowledges his love, and as he has the special privilege to have been the first creature who saw God, so likewise he has the special privilege to have been the first of God's creatures to love Mary the Mother of God.

And we will love thee, too, O blessed spirit! we will love thee, champion of Mary, our own sweet Mother, thy heavenly Queen. She is ours, she is a creature of flesh and blood; she sprang into existence, and lived her sweet life on earth before that God translated her to her proper place, above the bright spirits, her heavenly throne. We children of earth love and are proud of our Mother. We are glad that the Immaculate Virgin is the Angels' Queen, and we love God for His sweet wisdom and power. We love our good God, who has done all things well, who in such wondrous ways has united earth and heaven, who has made His Son the Son of Man, and our Mary the Angels' Queen.

Mary loved Michael when she lived on earth as well as now in heaven. We too must love that bright spirit. He will help us much, he will fight for us in all temptations, he will defend us in the day of battle, he will help us in our war for God, he will keep us as he kept the steadfast hosts of heaven, firm in our

allegiance to our God when His enemies assail
us and threaten us with destruction. Michael
will fight for his fair Queen in fighting for her
children; he will guard Mary's own as he
guarded her; and the only reward he asks is
that he may lead us to her throne, that he may
present us to his Queen as flowers of this earth,
well pleasing to the spotless Virgin, fit to
adorn her crown, because transformed by God's
grace into flowers of paradise; and such are
they who, though of this world, have kept
themselves unspotted from it, or who have
attained again to purity by penance, and thus
pleased God equally with those who have
never stained their baptismal innocence; such
are they who lived on this earth a simple,
humble life, like Mary their Mother; who
went about everywhere doing good, as Jesus
their Lord; who lived a life of love and labour,
a life so sweet in God's sight that the angels
might well envy their lot, for the angels cannot suffer for the love of God as we can, and
the life I have described cannot be without
suffering. They cannot *thus* delight God by a
life lived but for Him and His, a life of sacrifice, of unselfishness, of simplicity, in the
midst of difficulties and temptations which
they have not felt. May God increase the
number of such souls, living on this earth as

and thus Mary now gracious';
his love, and as he has the special .
have been the first creature w
likewise he has the special privil..
been the first of God's creatures :
the Mother of God.

And we will love thee, too, O ble--. ...
we will love thee, champion of Ma... .
sweet Mother, thy heavenly Quee...
ours, she is a creature of flesh and ti
sprang into existence, and lived her ...
on earth before that God transl..... .. ..
proper place, above the bright .. ..
heavenly throne.  We children of ...
and are proud of our Mother.
that the Immaculate Virgin is ...
Queen, and we love God for His .
and power.  We love our good God, ...
done all things well, who in su...
ways has united earth and heaven,
made His Son the S... ..
the Angels' Q... n.

May... ... Mi ...
as w... ... now ...
that bright s.
... fight

...s, so full of tender admiration...
... these loveable creatures of God...
... them, we wish our selfish
s loving as we enter-
Mary love them, how
r she is their Queen?
minds, and the thoughts
ederful to us. Mary
...ked in their midst on
them in heaven, she
...ey love to wait upon
...these. Sweet, gentle
these beautiful ones,
r, continually proclaim
... our so constantly,
Maria, Dei Genitrix
...culate Conception is
their favourite themes
...e to God; they never
the wonders of God in
h joy to them to adore
...cy, power, and all His
... see them manifested
...s in none other of His
...rld in herself," a world
...gels of God, together
love to look .... ...t
they m...

angels of earth, living but to live for love of Love.

St. Michael, guarding the Precious Blood, strengthen us by It. St. Michael, adoring the Precious Blood as It lay despised on the ground during the Passion, fill us with thy zeal for Its honour. St. Michael, lover of the Precious Blood in the Blessed Sacrament, make us constant lovers, make us unceasing adorers. May what was the life of our love, Jesus, be our life and love. Mary our Mother, first lover of the Precious Blood, make us share thy love. Amen.

---

## TENTH DAY.

### The Love of the Heart of our Lady for the Holy Angels.

Angels of God, beautiful bright spirits, do not our hearts grow light as we think of them and speak about them ? Do we not feel our hearts burn with love for the beautiful angels of love, those messengers from God, who bring us so many sweet messages from Him ? Oh yes, we surely do love you, holy angels, so pure, so lovely, so gentle, so compassionate

to us poor mortals, so full of tender solicitude.
We do love these loveable creatures of God,
and if we so love them, we with our selfish
natures, which hinder us loving as we otherwise should, how did Mary love them, how
does she love them now she is their Queen?
We ponder this in our minds, and the thought
grows more and more wonderful to us.  Mary
and the angels.  She walked in their midst on
earth, she reigns over them in heaven, she
commands them, and they love to wait upon
her, and perform her behests.  Sweet, gentle
Queen, surrounded by these beautiful ones,
who, clustering about her, continually proclaim
her blessed, who cry out so constantly,
"Sancta, sancta, sancta Maria, Dei Genitrix
et Virgo."  The Immaculate Conception is
their delight, it is one of their favourite themes
in their hymns of praise to God; they never
weary in contemplating the wonders of God in
Mary.  It is ever a fresh joy to them to adore
God's love, wisdom, mercy, power, and all His
various attributes, and see them manifested
and displayed in Mary as in none other of His
works.  "Mary is a world in herself," a world
of marvels that the angels of God, together
with the wise on earth, love to look upon, that
they may love it, that they may feed their

love of God upon it, that they may have fresh
store of beautiful thoughts about Him.

How did Mary love these angels whilst she
was on earth ? They visited her often. Tra-
dition tells us she had been long used to their
visits before Gabriel was sent from God with
his grand, his marvellous message. Yes, they
had visited Mary, flooding her pure soul with
unutterable delight. They were unlike anything on earth; they came to her straight
from her God, from the Most High, from the
Divine Author of her being, and she welcomed
them with glad delight. Her heart exulted,
her soul magnified her Lord, when she saw
their beauty. In a special manner did Mary
love the angel who had care of her, her guardian angel. Who was that highly favoured
being ? We know not. Some have supposed
it was the archangel Gabriel. It may have
been so, or it may have been one whom it
is reserved for us to meet and to know in
heaven, who wished here to be hidden, like
his Queen, and who begged that he might be
so. It is more than probable that Mary was
guarded by many angels. They were not
neglected by her, as ours are too often; they
were loved, and thanked, and honoured. And
this is a lesson Mary's own must learn from
her, to honour their guardian angel, to love

him, to treat with him familiarly, to reverence
his presence. For our own sakes we should
do this, if not from gratitude. They can so
greatly help us, if we will only let them. They
have special power from God to do so, for
God, who so greatly loves His own laws, who
regulates everything with such exquisite order,
helps us by certain mediums or secondary
agents, who are the channels of His grace to
us, to which, if we do not apply, we lose
the grace. Having appointed angels to
guard us, He will help us by their means.
He will help us by our patron saints more
than by others. This is what He has revealed to holy persons. We find in the life
of the Venerable Maria Taigi, that when once
praying for some one in whom she was much
interested, our Lord told her to pray to a certain saint for him, and it is related of her that
with charming familiarity she asked, " Why,
Lord, why more to this saint than to any
other ?" and received the answer that it was
because that saint was the patron of the person
for whom she was praying. There is much to
be thought of in this; we learn from it our
good God's love of order, without which nothing
can go on, nothing at least but confusion. As
in our own body each organ has to do its appointed work,—the eyes to see, the ears to

hear;—as in a well-appointed household the domestics have their appointed duties, without which the household would be in confusion; so through all creation each creature, inanimate, animate, or rational, has its office. So God ever acts, so thus applying this truth to the office of our guardian angels, we see that we have to look to them for help; and they can help us if we apply to them with faith, indeed they do ever help us whether we ask them or not; but as it is in other matters so in this, according to our dear Lord's words, "According to your faith be it done unto you." The help we shall receive from them will be greater in proportion to the faith we have in them. God's word likewise tells us that "He will have mercy on us, according to our trust in Him," and it is trusting in Him to trust His angels whom He has appointed as our guardians: so that those who have a lively faith, an active faith, a working faith, will receive help from their guardian angels that others will not, because they do not apply for it. In all our affairs, temporal as well as spiritual, our guardian angels will help us; they will whisper good thoughts, messages, as it were, from God; they will interest others in our behalf; they will warn us of dangers, and inspire us to pray when they see we are in danger. But alas! we are so deaf to their low gentle whispers and suggestions, they cannot make themselves heard; our hearts are in such a bustle, such an excitement, thinking of everything but the one thing necessary; they are so unlike the deep, still, calm of Mary's Heart. It was easy for angels to speak to her in their gentle whispers; they loved to hold converse with her, in a different way indeed from what we can ever hope or look for. It would be foolish and presumptuous to expect audibly to hear the voice of our guardian angel, as we may believe Mary did. Such is not the will of God, except in certain exceptional cases perhaps of saints; but He desires we should endeavour to live in their presence, to thankfully acknowledge the many interventions of grace we receive through their instrumentality. He desires we should seek help through the means He has established; and if He desires it, what more is needed to urge us at once to commence a lively, active, earnest devotion to the holy angels, and more particularly that one whom He has appointed to be our guardian? Thus shall we show ourselves to be the children of the Queen of Angels.

## ELEVENTH DAY.

### The Love of the Heart of our Lady for St. Joseph.

There is one love of Mary's Heart we might not think enough of; it was a great love and a peculiar one,—Mary's love for St. Joseph. Oh, pure, beautiful, conjugal love of Mary and Joseph, the dear, dear saint whom Mary so revered.  We have penetrated little into the secret recesses of Mary's Heart if we have not discovered its great love for St. Joseph, and if ours likewise do not love him in union with the Heart of our Mother.  What was the principal characteristic of Mary's love for St. Joseph ?  In what did it differ from many of the other loves that possessed her Heart?  In this, that with others they (even our Lord during a great part of His life) depended upon her, but she herself depended upon St. Joseph.  He was her spouse, her faithful guardian, and grateful indeed was Mary for the protector God had provided for her. Glad was she to rest upon him.  Mary, though indeed the "valiant woman," was not at all what would be called a strong-minded woman, as the people of the present day use that expression. The women of our times, clamouring for their rights, would have had no sympathy from her. Mary loved retirement and her quiet home duties. She loved to have one upon whom she could lean and whom she could defer to, one who would provide for her and shield her from the world. How could she expect to find such a one,—she who had resolved to remain ever a virgin? But there is nothing divine love cannot provide. It was to all appearances impossible, but nothing is impossible with God. We should have almost thought it necessary that an angel in form of man should have lived with her, and passed before the world for her spouse. But no; God chose St. Joseph ; God trusted him with the fair white lily of Jerusalem, and Mary in return poured upon him from her pure receptacle of love, her ineffably precious Heart, a love that she gave no other. No one shares with St. Joseph the love Mary bestowed upon him on earth, the love she now bears him in heaven.

Dear St. Joseph, our patron, our protector, we children of Mary turn to thee, we look up to thee, love thee, and entrust ourselves to thee. Take us under thy protection, most pure and holy saint; guard us from the dangers of the world; keep us innocent, without guile; may we be just in all things, as thou wert. In union with the Heart of Mary we consecrate ourselves to thee; do thou accept us children of Mary, who look to thee as our loving guardian and tender father. We love thee, dear holy St. Joseph, and trust thou wilt use thy powerful intercession with God on our behalf. Grant us thy blessing, and assist us now and at the hour of our death. Be with us then, dear saint, thou who in the hour of thy death didst make a sacrifice no other creature of earth has ever made.

Yes indeed, St. Joseph's death was happy, was peaceful, but likewise painful. And how was this? Had he not Jesus and Mary with him? Yes; but his death had this difference compared with that of any other soul upon this earth: they are not leaving God, they hope they are going to Him; St. Joseph was leaving Jesus and Mary, and though he knew full well he would be with the just, yet what must he have felt in being separated from our dear Lord and the sweet spouse he had guarded so tenderly,—Mary? None knew but thyself, dear saint, and yet no word of complaint escaped him; there was perfect submission to the will of God, placid resignation, entire

conformity to the divine will, which then
exacted so much from him. Should we not
have thought he would have asked to have
still remained to guard the fair white lily of
Jerusalem when she should be left alone in
this world, after Jesus had gone from it? Oh
no: St. Joseph, the "just one," was too perfect
for this. When God chose to use him he was
ready; he offered himself to Him, but if God
chose another, with holy Job he could say,
"The Lord gave, and the Lord hath taken
away: blessed be the name of the Lord."
Ah, what a flood of love and sorrow burst from
Mary's Heart as she saw that good just man
stretched out on his bed of death in such perfect patience and submission to the adorable
will of God. Mary reviewed the past in her
mind, with all its various scenes, its sorrows,
and its joys. They had lived a life of love to
God and man; they had lived ever united
together; they had lived with the one great
thought and anxiety to guard the treasure
confided to their care by the Eternal Father,
the precious Pearl of the Most Holy Trinity,
Jesus. Truly had St. Joseph fulfilled this
charge, the sacred office given him by the
Most High. He had had given him, to protect, to provide for, to cherish, the Virgin
Mother and the Child Divine, and truly far

before his own life had he guarded them, and then he lay down to die calmly. He did not think he was needed longer; he thought some one worthier, holier, better, would supply his place; he left all in the hands of God; he died; he left Jesus and Mary calmly, contentedly, happily and sorrowfully; sweetly, yet likewise with some grief of heart that he was not to be with Mary in the sorrowful hour he knew was yet to come, the hour of our Lord's Passion. He would have wished, if such had been God's will, to have been with Mary, to comfort the sorrowful Mother in her bitter pain; but such was not the will of God. Perhaps Mary had herself petitioned, in her sweet unselfishness, that he might not see the sad sights that she knew would be seen in after years in the streets of Jerusalem. However it may be, the hour had arrived for Joseph and Mary to part, and they parted in peace, and Mary turned to Jesus with that sweet Heart of hers full as she saw this death of the one so dear to her, and Jesus's Sacred Heart too was full as He thought of the other death—His own—that Mary was yet to witness. Jesus's gentle, sensitive Heart too felt, His loving Heart was likewise grieved.

Thus is God glorified by sacrifice, by sorrow, by suffering. Thus our sweet Mother gives example to all. Thus all states of life may look up to her; wives bereft of their husbands, mothers of their sons, all may look to Mary and learn from her. Let those who are bound so closely to her then learn her loves, look into her life, and live as she did.

> Loving spouse of dear St. Joseph,
> Make thy children love him too;
> May we think upon his goodness,
> May it soothe us in all woe.

## TWELFTH DAY.

### The Tobe of the Heart of our Lady for the Saints.

What an ardent longing there is in the Heart of our Mother to make her children saints. The saints are indeed to her other Christs; the saints are those who have worked their way to perfection, God working with them, through toil and trouble; the saints are those who have suffered; the saints are those who have loved. Love, suffering, sacrifice,—this is the motto of the saints. "Why should we not be saints, since we have hearts to love, and bodies to suffer?"*

* See "The Attributes of God, mirrored in the Perfections of Mary."

4

" We have to aim at becoming saints in
order to please God, not to please ourselves,
to please *our* God, to please the Mother of
God, our own Mother Mary, remembering that
saints are not those who are carried by the
power of God along the path to heaven, without any effort of their own; but those who
have laboriously tried to keep pace with God's
designs in their regard; those who have
found it difficult to follow as He goes before
them, but who nevertheless have followed, in
pain, weary, footsore, with heart-aching at
times, breathless, exhausted, and yet still
keeping on, never looking back, pressing ever
forward, counting not the toil, but hastening
as well as exhausted limbs and weary frame
would let them, toiling on after the Crucified,
striving to smile though weeping, looking
upon their Lord with eyes blinded with tears,
ever looking up and still following, rising after
every stumble, stretching out their hand to
Jesus even when they could not feel His
warm clasp in return, still trusting Him even
when darkness overtook them, still pressing on
regardless of pain, of falls, of wounds, of
weariness, of dereliction of soul, hoping, trusting, combating all who would lead them astray,
looking not back but ever forward.  Behold
God's saint, and behold God's justice in re-

warding. The touch from God, if I may so call it, the powerful grace is given in reward for these labours, that touch that changes sinners into saints, and that will surely come if we persevere; that great grace which is worth ten thousand years of toil. Then pursue your way, weary though you be; God will surely come; be ready for Him when He does. Accept from Him gratefully that wondrous help, which will so change you that your labours will not then be wearisome." Then indeed you will understand that His " yoke is easy and His burden light," when the soul lives no longer in itself, but God lives in it, and so possesses it that it seems to have no being of its own, but God is indeed all in all to it. Then all things teach that happy soul it is learning more of its Life and Love; but it does not learn from books. Books to the soul so closely united may be hindrances rather than helps. Sermons cannot tell that soul more of God than it learns in happy converse with Him; they cannot teach so much. Reading cannot help them any more than it would interest a traveller to read a description of a country he is travelling through. Sermons are like listening to a description of a person who is present, and whom you can look upon yourself and converse with intimately.

These simple yet wise and happy souls are indeed the favoured ones of earth : they are intensely happy, but rarely if ever is this state attained to but through terrible trials, terrific struggles, entire mortification of will ; but if those knew who have to go through this terrible desert, if they knew the fair, the lovely land of unchanging peace beyond, if they knew that on this earth even they may taste that sweet, joyous, constant peace of God, unknown to so many, who if they had but once tasted it, would acknowledge that all the pleasures they have ever enjoyed were as nothing to this joy of God; if they, I say, knew this, they would surely have courage. Then do you who are now suffering take heart, be brave, be courageous, offer up generously your pains, both of mind and body. Thank God for them on earth ; but thank Him as you may, you will never thank Him as He deserves to be thanked, and as you will thank Him hereafter in heaven, for this most precious gift, the gift of well-borne suffering, which will bring you so close to the Crucified in heaven, which will make you loved so dearly by the Mother above all mothers, our own dear Mother Mary. She will press you close to her breast, sweet Mother. You will give her great joy, and who would not wish to give joy to the tender, gentle Mother who suffered so for us? Who would not wish to repay her care for us, her pain and trouble endured for us? We will do this, sweet Mother. Thy own shall be saints. We will by God's grace be saints ourselves, and influence all around us to become saints likewise, for the saints do not go to heaven alone, they take others with them; so we shall, if we become saints ourselves, make others saints also, and then truly shall we be doing our Mother's work. Truly shall we be then her most dear children, nourished at her breast, fed with the milk of her love, sweetly inebriated with the joy of God.

Yes; on this earth the saints commenced their heaven. There are three states in this world as well as in the next. There is heaven, at least a foretaste of it; there is purgatory; there is hell, alas! unfortunately already begun in some souls. We must most of us go through purgatory in the next life, before we reach heaven; and so in this we have the purgative state to go through before we arrive at the happy state the saints arrived at. But we most of us stand still in the purgative way, we dread the fiery ordeal we must go through ere we can join the company of saints on earth. But it is an unreasonable dread. It

is hard enough, truly ; the saints cry out, with
the King of saints, as the hour of their passion
arrives, " If it be possible, let this chalice pass
from me ;" but the "fiat" was still in their
hearts, and they drank that chalice, they went
bravely through their crucifixion, though
human nature trembled, and their hearts
seemed at times to fail them, and they could
well nigh have given up, and say they could
bear no more, it was too hard, unkindness of
friends, desertion of those they loved best,
death of those they leaned upon, failure where
they thought success was sure, apparently
irresistible temptations, seeming desertion by
God Himself; but still, when breathless they
have passed through the waste, they look
back, and from their hearts chant a glad " Te
Deum" to the good God who Himself carried
them through, for they know without Him they
would have lain down and died on the way.

Take now one glimpse of heaven, where the
joyful Mother is seated, surrounded by her
many children of every tribe and clime. They
are basking now in her sunshine, calm, happy,
content, they who were once on earth so sorrowful, so sad, so sorely afflicted. Mary bends
over them with her beauteous smile; she
looks upon them as none but mothers look, and
her smile rewards them for their labours on

earth, for their broken heart, their bruised, crushed soul. But they have another reward; they, too, in their turn, seem to be mothers; they are surrounded by souls, who cluster round, who cling to them with love, proclaiming that they owe their happiness to those blessed ones. Mother of Saints, thou who hast formed so many of God's most cherished ones, thou hast received us as thy very own, we leave ourselves docilely in thy hands, to form us at thy will; we put ourselves entirely into thy care; we will not stray from the path of the saints, but will steadily persevere, ever recollecting that one saint pleases God and gives Him more glory, does more good, than a whole nation of ordinary Christians. Therefore we, wishing to please God, wishing to give Him glory, wishing to do good and to save souls, wishing to be most dear cherished children of Mary, are resolved to be saints, we will be saints. May God in His mercy help our endeavours, and so strengthen us and bless us, that, having once put our hands to the plough, we may never look back, but may proceed on our way prosperously.

## THIRTEENTH DAY.

### The Love of the Heart of our Lady for Sinners.

Do we value souls? Have we the slightest idea how beautiful, how very beautiful they are? Do we realize the fact that the loveliest thing we ever saw on earth cannot be compared to the lovely soul we bear within us? If we do consider that the likeness of the beautiful God is imprinted on the soul, if we do meditate on the priceless value of the soul, if we in our degree love souls, we shall then the better understand the wondrous love of Mary for poor sinners, those who are entangled in the snares of Satan, those whom he has entrapped, those who unhappily are bound down by him, and who so need a helping hand to assist them, and who indeed ought to receive that kind Samaritan help when they so need it. Our Lord has given us the example of the Samaritan, but how few practise the lesson it teaches. Then again there is the father of the prodigal, whom we have to imitate. But above all there is our Mother Mary, our model, next to our Lord Himself, in love for sinners. Ah, if we but saw her, if we on earth could but see the anxiety, the thought, the care, the continual watchful love of our Mother the Queen of Heaven, we should love herself far more, and we should likewise love poor sinners more. Why do we not? We talk about it, we say we do; we often have grand thoughts about the conversion of sinners; but come nearer home, some member of your family offends you wrongfully, treats you unjustly,—what about your love for sinners then? How do you win that sinner back to God? There is the opportunity for you to put in practice your grand resolutions. You had better put by, for the time at least, your theory of praying for the whole world, and pray for that one poor sinner practically, and your prayer will have power, since you are the sufferer, the sin is against yourself. It may be a very grievous offence, the person who committed it may be most unloveable; but Christ died for that soul. It is now in the meshes of Satan's net; no wonder it has disagreeable qualities that make it appear despicable to you. Now is the time for putting your love for souls to the test, now is the time to see if your apparent virtue is really solid. Oh, think that hundreds of years ago a dying Saviour looked upon that soul and longed to embrace it, thirsted for it, loved it as none but Jesus has ever loved.

That soul was precious to Him; if it has sinned, it is Jesus who is injured by the sin. You only think of yourself, you should think of Him, the loving Saviour of that soul, you should think of His anxiety to save it. Have you done this in the past? and if not, will you not for the future? Will you not be Mary-like? Will you not turn to God, telling Him of your own indignation against yourself? Will you not turn to Him, and plead for forgiveness, doing some penance, however slight it may be; though slight, God will accept the spirit that offers it more than the actual suffering endured. Will you not now resolve to offer your Mother this resolution you now make of loving sinners, and of loving them, not in word, but in *deed* and in *truth?* This is a great, great love of Mary's Heart, the love of sinners. Jesus came for sinners, therefore Mary came for them. Jesus is Saviour. Saviour of whom? Of sinners. Mary is Mother of the Saviour, Mary has to co-operate in saving sinners. Jesus shed His Blood, and died for each single sinner who would ever live upon this earth. Mary suffered and sorrowed for each one, she yearned after all, as Christ died for all. Let us, then, be in union with her; let us, too, love sinners; let us strive with might and main to save them;

let us ever remember that it is by love we shall do this, by practical working love, by the kind word, by the good advice, by the good example, by patience, by compassion, by sacrifice, by the sacraments, by the many ways with which we can bring the Precious Blood to be applied to their souls. Mother, sweet Mother, enkindle in our hearts thy love for souls, thy love for sinners, poor tempted sinners, that we too, loving them, may bring them to Jesus, may bring them to Mary. Thus shall we show that we have God's Spirit in us, that the Spirit of Jesus and Mary lives within us, that we are truly children of the God of Love.

Oh, that wondrous love of Mary for poor sinners. We linger over it, thinking what we cannot say, what we cannot write ; but resting on our Mother's breast, we feel more than we can express. We would save the whole world; not one soul shall be lost if we can prevent it. We think of the heathens in far-off lands, and burn to save them. But, as I have said before, let us first begin at home ; let us preach love of others by word and example ; let us avoid detraction as we would the devil himself ; let us have a good word for every one ; let us be silent upon what cannot be excused, let us strive to put in practice our

dear Lord's command of loving one another as
He has loved us.    If we did this as we should
do it, what apostles should we not be.    How
the world would flock into the Church, how
we should indeed show that we are the true
followers of Christ; but we do not do it.    Our
Lord is slighted because we slight our neighbour; our Lord is not loved because we do
not love others.    Souls drop into hell daily,
hourly, because no kind hand is put out to
save them.    Ah me, what a sad, sad thought
is this, what an awful thought:  there may
be souls in hell now whom we might have
saved.    Let us now make up for the past; let
Mary's own go forth upon their mission of
love; let them spread love wherever they go;
let them daily draw near to their Mother's
Heart, to increase their own love, and then
pour it forth upon others; let them be angels
of love, bringing messages of love; let them
be instruments God can use at any moment,
because they are ever full of love, and God's
blessing will be upon them, and they will
know He dwells with them, they will know
that they are fulfilling His will, because
charity is the fulfilling of the law, the law of
love that our dear Lord came from heaven to
preach, but to whose sweet preaching so few
listen.    But, Mother, thy own will listen to

their Teacher, and thou wilt keep us in God's love, in which we can only abide by loving our neighbour, for so the apostle of love tells us, " If any man say, I love God, and hateth his brother, he is a liar; for he that loveth not his brother whom he seeth, how can he love God whom he seeth not ?"

---

## FOURTEENTH DAY.

### The Love of the Maternal Heart of Mary for the Holy Souls.

How dear to Mary are the souls in purgatory. Some say she herself visits them in their place of suffering. This must indeed comfort them. Methinks we would willingly suffer a great many years to see the sweet face of our Mother, with the maternal light of love in her eyes, with which she ever looks upon her children, but more especially upon those who are in suffering. Oh, how great the joy to see Mary once, to be in her presence, to hear the sound of her voice. Mother, if you visit your children in purgatory, is it only that you may comfort them, or is it likewise that you may add to their pain, by causing

them such grief when you leave them, and
they cannot follow you, that thus by increas-
ing their pain you may enable them sooner to
join you in heaven?   Once to see you, and
then to leave you.   Mother, thou art with us
on earth.   Bending over thy own, they feel
and acknowledge thy presence; thy company
is sweet; thou whisperest sweet words to
them; thou makest known secret, hidden
things; thou revealest thyself in so many ways
that they cannot imagine life without thee.
But at death dost thou leave them?  Are they
who are suffering temporary punishment deprived of thee ?   Is it part of their punishment to be kept from thee ?  Those who have
have lived so closely with thee on earth, dost
thou withdraw from at death?   Mother, if so
indeed we fear purgatory, truly we will  pray
for those who are in it.   Yes, it is a holy and
wholesome  thought  to  pray  for  the   dead.
Those who have been so happy with thee on
earth, even in the midst of sorrow, may now
be weeping and crying to us, " Have pity on
me, have pity on me, at least you my friends,
for the hand of the Lord hath touched me, the
sweet light of Mary's countenance is hidden
from me."

Prayers will bring them relief, but more
especially indulgences.  Indulgenced prayers

may be called prayers steeped more deeply
than others in the Precious Blood of Jesus.
Be most earnest in gaining indulgences.
Every day strive to gain many. Have a
habit of using little indulgenced prayers,
even though it be only, " My Jesus, mercy;"
" Sweet Heart of Mary, be my salvation."
Mary's own may and should strive to gain
several plenary indulgences every day. Those
who wear the Blue Scapular,—as all should,
and indeed all the Scapulars, since every
grace that can be obtained by Mary's own
should be obtained ; their work needs all ;
(it is more than a matter of life and death;)—
those, I say, who wear the Blue Scapular of
the Immaculate Conception can, by repeating
six Our Fathers, Hail Maries, and Glorias, in
honour of the Blessed Trinity, the Immaculate
Conception, and for the intentions of the holy
Father, gain many and very great indulgences. Assist the holy souls. Help your
children in pain and suffering. Show yourselves true mothers. There is an indulgence
for saluting each other with "Blessed be Jesus
Christ," with its accompanying response,
" Blessed for ever." It is a good custom to
do so. Help the holy souls, and they will
greatly help you ; do works of charity, such
as giving alms for that intention. " But I say

to you, make to yourselves friends of the
mammon of iniquity, that when you fail, they
may receive you into everlasting dwellings."

The Queen of Heaven, their Mother, desires
that her children of earth should help her
children in purgatory.  She desires that the
angels of heaven may whisper with exceeding
joy, " How these Christians love one another;
how are Christ's children one in the union of
charity and love."  If we are really happy,
secure by being near the warm loving Heart
of our Mother, we ourselves shall be warmed
by it, we shall be inflamed with some little of
its warmth of love, and we too shall love these
dear holy souls.  How tenderly we think of
them.  They seem to us so child-like, so
beautifully simple, so patiently, cheerfully
suffering, so intensely humble.  God bless
them !  God ever love them !  Rejoicingly
we think that God has already blessed them
with an everlasting blessing.  They will
indeed be eternally loved by that Divine
Lover of souls, to obtain and to keep whose
love it is well worth while to give up all
things.  We too will strive to abide ever in
Thy love, dear God ; and we shall surely do so
if we keep ever in our Mother's company, loving all her loves, doing ever what she would
have us do.  And this is one of the many works

of love the Heart of Mary desires from her
children on earth, in the midst of their own
struggles, trials, and temptations, not to forget the suffering souls in purgatory. This
desire, then, of our Mother we will give to
her. Sweet Mother, we live to do thy will
and wish, and to breathe to heaven thy sweet,
earnest, loving prayer for thy suffering children. Draw us nearer to thy breast; keep
us from straying far from thee; let us not
grow dry and hard by seeking self. Banish
self-love from our hearts, that pure and un-
defiled we may walk ever in God's presence,
most pleasing in His sight. Many of the
holy souls have a peculiar and special love
from Mary, because they are the fruit of a
broken heart, a bruised soul. They owe their
salvation, (the special grace that brought
them to receive the Precious Blood upon their
souls, without which they would not have
been saved,) they owe this to the sorrowful
Mother, and there is a special yearning fond-
ness in her Heart for them; they are indeed
her very own. So should it be with us too, in
our measure; we too should have children in
purgatory; we should love to think we have
prayed, sorrowed, and suffered for souls; and
trusting in God's promises, in His grand
mercy, we should hope, and glorify Him by

our hope, that thus we have saved many, and if it indeed be so, then they are in a certain sense ours; we have been more than mother to them, we have given them the eternal life of heaven. Therefore let us continue our motherly office, let us pray until we have our children out of purgatory into heaven. They too will pray for us; their prayers are most powerful with God, perhaps for the reason that their prayers are so unselfish, and because they pray whilst suffering, which makes prayer so efficacious. Try a novena for the relief of the holy souls; pray for them habitually, whether in novena or otherwise, and you will soon discover its efficacy. The holy souls are so grateful, they are so loving, they long so to help their benefactors. What a happy meeting we may hope to have one day in heaven with souls we have thus benefitted. God grant we may persevere in prayer for them.

# FIFTEENTH DAY.

## The Love of the Heart of our Lady for the Apostles.

Mary indeed loved those favoured ones of Christ, those privileged ones, who were chosen from amongst men to be the familiar friends and companions of the Son of Man, who walked with Jesus, ate with Him, slept with Him. O most enviable companionship. Look upon the Son of God made Man, as He walks through the corn-fields, or along the roads and streets of Galilee or Judea, with these chosen ones. How our love for our Lord grows as we watch Him in His sweet simplicity, with His beautiful condescension, His gentle humility, that humility that was so perfect because it was so natural, practised without the slightest effort, not as we often see in those who, though really condescending to their inferiors, and who strive to be kind and affable, still show and make others feel their superiority. Not so with our Lord; there was indeed unspeakable dignity and majesty in His outward demeanour, but combined with marvellous gentleness, and suavity, and sim-

plicity, which put every one who conversed
with Him entirely at their ease.    How
Mary loved to watch Jesus with His apostles ;
how her whole being was flooded with love, .
which her simplicity, her love of all that is
quiet, unaffected, her utter aversion to what is
extraordinary, or has even the appearance of
exaggeration, hindered her from manifesting
in some exterior way, by some grand outburst
of admiration, some wonderful display of
enthusiasm, as she saw and watched Jesus
with His apostles.    And how she loved them
too.    Let us view Mary, gentle, sweet, in the
midst of the apostles.    How great must have
been their love for their fair spotless Virgin-
Mother, and how eager were they to make her
feel how much they loved her in their simple
rude way, for they had not been bred in courts ;
but though rude and simple, inspired by
reverence the most profound.    Mary repaid
their love, well indeed whilst Jesus was on
earth, but still more when He had left it.
Then she had to hide her own sorrow that she
might comfort them ; they looked to her for
it.    John was ever with her, he who was
simple, loving, caressing, as a little child, who
had leaned his head upon the bosom of Jesus,
came to his Mother, and resting his head upon
Mary's breast, let the silent tears of grief for

his lost Master fall slowly from his full heart, and thus gained strength from Mary to bear his exile. There came Peter, too, who, throwing himself on his knees by her side, hiding his face for shame, sobbed aloud in his bitter anguish at the thought of having denied his Lord, and craved her pity and forgiveness. They all came with their various trials, temptations, and troubles, and were comforted. St. Paul, who had not known his Lord on earth, sought to know Him from His gentle Mother. And Mary loved this task. Jesus had left her the apostles to console, to comfort, to sustain, even to train. They looked up to her, they listened to her words. The visible presence of their Lord, which had been such a support and comfort, was withdrawn; but they had with them the loving Mother's Heart that beat within that fair frame, and they loved her presence. There was something so like Jesus about her that they could hardly account for it; they would speak of it to each other, and wonder at it, but it brought their Master to their minds, and they sought her company, and Mary ever welcomed them.

The Holy Ghost came upon them in the company of Mary; they were continuing in prayer with *Mary the Mother of Jesus*, when the Holy Spirit descended to change them entirely from what before they had been into supernatural men, to empty them of their own spirit, and to fill them with the Holy Spirit of God. It was with Mary and in her company that this grand work was accomplished, and how did Mary rejoice in the growth of grace in their souls; how happy it made her to see them growing into the likeness of the Incarnate One; with what joy did she watch the workings, the operations of the Holy Spirit in them; with what anxious Motherly love did she not pray for them, that they might use their graces well and be faithful. What grief of soul was hers when she saw them in danger, when she saw the snares of the evil one surrounding them; how earnestly did she pray to avert the evil; how she watched, as having to give an account, since by the ordinance of Jesus she was their Mother, and therefore she had to do a Mother's part by them : and a Mother's part, what is it but to combine ever with all the natural means that can be used, constant, earnest, unwavering, unwearying prayer? This an ordinary good mother would do. How earnest, then, must Mary have been in the performance of this part of her office. She prayed even for poor Judas, and but for his own malice and despair her prayers would

have saved him. He pierced her Heart as
she saw the magnificent graces Jesus had
given him so abused. How earnestly she
prayed for Peter in his fall; how she rejoiced
with him in his repentance; how she, like
Jesus, showed him special love and consideration. As our dear Lord had singled him out
after His resurrection with such tender
thoughtfulness, saying, "Go, tell My disciples
and *Peter*," so Mary likewise gave him marks
of special love, as we do to those who have
injured us, for fear lest they may think that
we have not forgotten their offence.

Sweet Mother, how dear thou art to us.
We see thee in the midst of the apostles, and
learn to love thee better. As we look upon
thy various loves, and see thee with all thy
grand prerogatives, with all thy magnificent
graces, commencing on earth with the first
great grace of thy Immaculate Conception,
and arriving at their fulness in heaven by thy
final crowning as Queen of Heaven, we have
often thought of thy wonders, and praised God
for His goodness to thee; but our hearts burn
more as we see thee so simple, so humble, so
Motherly, all that we can imagine or conceive
most beautifully sweet and gentle. Thanks
be to our God for His gift of thee. Mary,
grant us grace to remove from our minds all

impediments, all distractions, that would hinder us from dwelling in thought with thee, and living in thy company as children with a much-loved Mother, who love to be ever with their mother, as all love to be with those they love.

We must indeed try to keep in our Mother's company, by our thought of her; we must keep in her company by striving to imitate her; by thinking of her we shall learn to love as she loved; by looking upon her in her sweet, humble, domestic life, we shall learn to do as she did, and thus endear ourselves to God, and be beloved by Him as His most cherished children. So may it be, dear Lord, and so may we persevere, that having lived in Mary's company in this world, we may live in it for ever with Jesus, His angels, and saints, for all eternity in that world where God is reigning in all His glory, glory which Mary's children will surely see, and love, and rejoice in with somewhat of the love and joy with which the fair Mother of God rejoices as she beholds His glory. In that glory we too, who now know ourselves to be so cold, will then to the full with new hearts rejoice. We shall see there God's saints, and rejoice in their joy. We shall see there those apostles whom Mary so loved, and we too shall love them

with some little of our Mother's love, and
they will return our love, and will rejoice that
we had grace to follow in their footsteps,
being imitators of them as they were of Christ.

———

## SIXTEENTH DAY.

### The Love of the Heart of our Lady for the Holy Father.

Do we love the Vicar of Christ, our dear
holy Father, the representative of our Lord to
us? Is there a special, a peculiar, a supernatural love in our hearts for the one who is
so truly the father of our souls on earth, to
whom God has granted such great powers?
If we have not this love then are our hearts
not attuned to Mary's, for from the time she
saw her son, the repentant Peter, ascend the
papal throne, and rejoiced with him in the
greatness of his office, so to the present day
each Vicar of Christ has had a special love and
prayer from the Heart of Mary, has been
watched over with special loving, maternal
care, and prayed for with her most ardent
prayers. She would have her children likewise true devoted children of the Vicar of
5

Christ; she would have them daily watch in prayer for him; she would have them anxious, eager followers of him, zealous in his cause, all together united to protect him, to stand up for his rights, ready to fight and lay down their lives for him if needful; she would have her children ever keep in harmony with the Holy See, that is to say, to take their every tone of thought from it, to be ready to give up their own views, not only when it is absolutely necessary, under pain of mortal sin and excommunication, as in matters of faith; but even in regard to matters where there is no question of sin, to endeavour that our own line of thought and conduct may harmonize with that pursued by the holy Father. He is our guide, our leader; the Holy Ghost with him, guiding and assisting him, he is infallible in matters of faith, when he addresses the whole Church from his chair of truth; he is marvellously enlightened in matters that are not of faith; he pursues a supernatural course that little minds with narrow views may not be able at once to see and understand; his patience is something divine, and the great strength of the Holy See lies in this very patience, which the impatient world cannot comprehend, but nevertheless cannot help admiring. Men of the world see the grand

patience, the marvellous hope of the See of
Peter, and they feel that it is not of this
earth, they see it is something supernatural,
but they do not understand it, it is a puzzle to
them. They do not see that the holy Pontiff
is leaning upon his beloved Lord; he, the
visible head of the Church, knowing well that
he is but the representative of the invisible
Head, Jesus; knowing that he ·is an instru-
ment in the hands ·of God. He knows that
the Church entrusted to his care is founded
upon a rock, and he waits his time, or rather
the time appointed by his Lord. But here
we must notice again what we have remarked
elsewhere, that though Providence rules
supreme, and appoints Its own times and
seasons, still God expects us to do our part;
God expects those in power to do their part;
God expects the lowliest and least of His
Church to do each their individual part, to use
whatever natural means may lie within their
power to further the interests of His cause, as
for instance, a vote, a word in season, and the
numerous and various ways we have of showing that we, the members of Christ's Body,
are united with the head, that we are true and
loyal followers of our Lord, and that we love
His representative, our holy Father the Pope,

for such union made manifest to the world is itself a tower of strength.

Our Mother in heaven, to whom we have given ourselves as her faithful children, desires that her own should prove themselves her true children by their allegiance to the Holy See; should band themselves together, united in prayer; and should the opportunity arrive, united in action. Thus shall we please our Mother, thus shall we endear ourselves to her loving Heart, for we shall be in union with it, and true love always leads to union, and union should mean being united by being alike, alike in thought, in intention, in desire. Let us, then, be like Mary, and let the loves of our hearts be like the loves of her Heart; so shall we be most dear children of God, so shall we become like the Son of His love, and this is all perfection, to become like the Incarnate One, Jesus the Son of God.

---

## THE PEOPLE'S PRAYER FOR THEIR PASTOR, THE HOLY FATHER.

The hearts of Thy people cry unto Thee, O Lord. Let Thine ears be attentive to the voice of their supplication, pleading for their Pastor and chief Bishop. The souls of many

rest upon him, dear Lord; be mindful of Thy
great mercy, and give him help who has so
great need of Thy assistance if he would save
the souls committed to his care. Give him
those helps, spiritual and temporal, of which
he has need in his arduous work; give him
good helpers to work in Thy vineyard, of which
he is pastor, and for which he will be responsible to Thee in the day of judgment. Mary,
spouse of the Holy Ghost, obtain that a very
special light from the Holy Spirit may direct
him in all his ways. Mother of Jesus, and
our Mother, present our prayer for our Holy
Father before the throne of God; plead by
thy Maternal Heart with thy Son. Jesus will
not refuse the prayer from the Heart of His
Mother. Holy Saints, we honour you through
the Heart of Jesus; join our prayer. Holy
Angels, bring graces from on high, and obtain
for His Vicar and us that we may fight the
good fight to the end, and that pastor and
people, having been one on earth, may come
at length to the one only true and living God,
to live together for ever in joy and peace in
heaven.

The Bishop of Nottingham grants forty days' Indulgence and a special blessing to all who recite this
Prayer. People should also recite a like Prayer for
their Bishop, who is the representative of the Holy
Father to them.

## SEVENTEENTH DAY.

### The Love of our Lady for the Church.

The angels and the saints in heaven are looking upon something on this earth that is wondrously beautiful, the object of the Eternal Father's complacency, something divine, something so marvellously fair, because it is like to Jesus the beloved Son of God. What is this? What could it be but the spouse of Christ, His Church. Mother Church, fruitful and virginal; Mother Church, dear art thou to the Heart of God, dear to us. Thou art following thy Lord, treading in His steps, more beautiful, more loveable now in the time of thy passion, as was thy Master. We love thee, holy Church, " we will be true to thee till death," and we will, by God's grace, be thy glory in heaven. We are members of this Church, we are followers of Christ, we are true Christians; but we often live immersed in business and cares, either our own or of others, and we cannot get out of our petty worries and distractions, and take a broad view of God and of the works of God.

If, however, we keep close to our Mother's Heart, to learn its loves, we must of necessity

love the holy Church, we shall be devoted to
it, we shall with might and main strive to
draw all to love it too. We shall reverence
its slightest orders; we shall esteem it, as it
is in truth, the work of God, the voice of God!
We must love it as our life, and dearer than
our life, for honoured should we be if we could
lay down our lives for it. It is beautiful, it is
divine, it is immortal; it is founded, watered,
cemented by the Blood of Jesus; it is informed
by the Holy Spirit as its very soul, our dear
Lord is Himself its Head, and therefore Mary
is its Mother. Yes, Mary is Mother of the
Church; she is Mother of all Christians
individually, and so of the entire body; but
also of the entire body in its corporate capacity,
as being the mystical body of Christ. And
how dearly does she love the Church! What
great part she took in the forming of it,
bringing its Author into this world, working
with Him in the grand work of its formation,
assisting at His death for love of it, helping
and encouraging its members after the death
of Jesus. "The widowed Church leant upon
her then," and well did she sustain its weight,
well did she work in her simple Mary-like
way, instructing the young catechumens, consoling the apostles in their many trials, and
all so quietly, so unobtrusively, so differently

from the way in which some good people work
in these days. " How much might be done to
help our over-worked priests by those who
have the goodwill and the right intention, and
are single-hearted, looking only to God's glory
and the honour of His Church. But the lay
help often sought by our hard-working priests
too often proves a source of annoyance and
trouble to them, the pious ladies whom they
engage being often fussy, given to take offence,
and talkative to a degree." But how much
work might be done by quiet Mary-like souls,
souls loving all Mary's loves, souls who have
imbibed her spirit, souls who love to tread in
her footsteps, and walk in her ways, and to
imitate her example. If our priests had such
helpers as these, how much more good might
they not do, what labour they might be saved,
how God's Church might be extended.

Dear indeed was God's Church to Mary;
happy would she have been to have given her
life for it. But did she not do more when she
offered the life of Jesus? And now in heaven
the Church is still more beautiful to Mary,
since she views it in the light of God's love.
Indeed the Church is like herself,—it is virginal. Though in the world, it is not of the
world. In all that is essential it is indepen-
dent of the world, though it needs to use the

things of the world in the work it has to do.
It receives its life from God, it leans upon
Him alone. Those who are animated by God's
Spirit may indeed assist it, and glorify it, and
adorn it, but it has its life from God alone,
and it imparts that life to others. It is indeed
a fruitful mother. Springing into life from its
bosom, day by day, hour by hour, are countless multitudes, but it is from God it receives
this power to increase and multiply, to give
birth, a new and heavenly birth to its children.
It is like Mary in this,—it is a mother, because the power of the Most High has overshadowed it. Again, it is like Jesus, and
Mary's love for it resembles her love for Jesus
Himself, and blessed spirits above exclaim in
wonder, "Quæ est ista?" as they watch the
progress of the Church on earth. The saints
love to look from their abode above, their safe
haven in heaven, and follow the Church as,
like its Master, it treads its weary way onward
through the ages, from its first hidden life in
the catacombs, as Jesus came forth from
Bethlehem and Nazareth; and now that they
see it on its way to Calvary, more beautiful
does it become in their sight. Are we not
now nearing Calvary? and what lesson should
we learn from that? A lesson of fear lest we
should forsake our Lord, as His nearest and

dearest did at that time. We love holy
Church, we would die for it; and so said St.
Peter to our Lord, but he left Him, he forsook
Him, he denied Him. How many whom we
thought saints have left our Lord already in
these sad times of ours. God grant we may
not see more. Let us pray for them as Mary
did for Peter, let us bring them back to the
feet of Jesus; and let us likewise pray for
ourselves, that we may stand firm. If we are
with our Mother we are safe. St. John and
the holy women went to Calvary under the
protection of Mary. Let us join their company, let us keep in the company of Mary,
let us dread to leave it as we would dread to
forsake Jesus, and we shall be safe. Our
Mother will throw her mantle round her children, she will guard them, because they have
trusted themselves to her; she will protect
them, she will guard them for Jesus, whose
Holy Spirit brought them to her tender care.

But our Mother knows that these times are
bad, she knows that we need more than ever
now to pray if we would persevere; therefore
must we pray, each individual soul for itself,
alone with its Lord; the soul and its Saviour
must hold loving converse. Has the soul its
fears, its doubts, its perplexities? Let it tell
them to Jesus; He will encourage it, en-

lighten it, and dispel its doubts. He has brought us to His Church as our ark of refuge; He would have us live and not die. If we plead we shall persevere; but indeed we need prayer, or we may fall as some around have fallen; we may leave God's Church, to our own eternal ruin, but this will never be if we pray; through all temptations we shall cling to her as the one ark of salvation. Mary, Mother of the Church, help us who cry to thee in our distress and trouble. Mary leads the soul to Jesus that it may pour forth its prayer for perseverance.

## THE SOUL'S PRAYER FOR PERSEVERANCE.

"Jesus, my life, grant me this grace of perseverance. By the love Thou hast for the Heart of Thy Mother, my Mother, hear me." And Jesus bends, all attentive, to the human voice so dear to Him; and as from His Sacred Heart flowed the stream of Precious Blood, so now there is ever flowing a stream of precious gifts and graces, and they who draw nearest to that divine source receive most plenteously from the sacred stream. "Jesus, inspire into the hearts of many this holy vocation, that as spouses of Thy holy suffering Heart they may press, and plead, and entreat Thee without

ceasing, and induce Thee to bestow the mercy
Thou lovest to bestow, that their united
pleading may draw from Thee what the Heart
of Thy Mother desires, what she bids her
children pray for,—mercy. Jesus, mercy;
my Jesus, mercy. But, O Lord my God, not
only do Thou inspire souls with this holy
vocation, but grant them likewise, dear Lord,
I pray Thee, the grace to persevere. Can it
be, O God, that ever one who has been once
united to Thee on the cross, lifted in Thy
warm embrace away from the world which
lies beneath with its vanities and sins,—can
it be, my God, that one, even one, would ever
descend from that cross, and leave Thee, O
Jesus, who art that soul's true Love, to become an adulteress, to embrace the world and
its sin and vanity? Oh God, remove this
fear far from me: my heart is full of grief and
anxiety for Thee. Jesus, I pray now on earth
for myself and others; grant that I may one
day pray in heaven for those on earth. Let
not this be, O Jesus, let not this be, I beseech
Thee; hearken to the words of my mouth:
put forth Thy strong right hand; show Thy
might and power; suffer not any who have
come to Thee ever to be faithless and leave
Thee, leave Thy Church that Thou so lovest.
Oh God, would that I could answer for all,

and say, ' Lord, by Thy grace this shall never
be.' My God, I will never leave Thee ; I am
Thine, Thine only, Thine alone. Mother,
answer thou for me, answer thou for thine."

And the whisper of Jesus comes sweet to
the soul, " If thou didst but know, in this thy
day, the things that are for thy peace in
heaven. Thy queen, My Mother, stands at
My right hand, clothed about with variety ;
ever more and more beautiful does that vesture
of My Mother become, adorned with fresh
flowers transplanted from My earthly paradise, My Church; but the fairest blossoms of
earth, that will bloom for ever with Mary in
heaven, are those who are *Mary's* own, for
therefore are they *Mine*."

---

## EIGHTEENTH DAY.

### The Love of the Heart of our Lady for Priests.

If there is one upon this earth in whom our
Lady would wish to live, of whose soul and
heart she would desire to be entire mistress, it
is that most favoured of human beings, God's
priest. Yes, the office of priest is indeed
Mary-like. Happy are those holy ones who
understand and endeavour to perfect the

resemblance, and to make their lives a copy of our Lady's, who in the midst of their many and various duties lead an interior supernatural life in as close a conformity to Mary's life as human infirmity will permit. Do we reverence Christ's priests as we should? Another question,—Do even priests themselves value, esteem their office as it is to be esteemed? Hardly, perhaps; it is scarcely possible in this world. Saints have been enlightened to understand it, and have shrunk in holy dread from its wondrous dignity and terrible obligations. We are told that we should salute a priest before an angel if we met both together. The angel has not the power to do what the priest can do: the angel cannot call God from heaven, but the priest can and does daily.

Our Lady was the first who called God from heaven by her word, "Fiat mihi secundum verbum tuum." The priest has succeeded her, and does what she did. Mary loves to perform again this wondrous work in the person of her "own" priests; she loves to live again in them, and again to perform her motherly offices to Jesus by the hands of her priest.

The Mother with her Divine Child. The Mother who with such reverence wrapped in swaddling clothes and laid Him in a manger,

seems to live again in the priest of God with
his Lord, with the Sacred Host laid on the
linen corporal, resting in the tabernacle,
where he places Him. It has been almost as
a rule, in the instances we read of, that our
Lord has miraculously manifested His divine
presence in the Sacred Host under the form
of an Infant. See the priest bending over
the Host, you see the Mother bending over
her Child; see the priest with the Host raised
to heaven, you see the Mother raising her
Infant to the Eternal Father; see the priest
bowed low to receive his Lord, you see Mary
with her Infant pressed to her breast.

You may say this analogy applies in some
degree to all Christians. It is true, but to
none does it apply as it does to the priest.
Our Lady's priests understand this well; they
feel our Lady working in them, animating
them with her spirit, filling them with her
loves, lending them her heart. They are
indeed happy men, privileged beings. And
what should Mary's children do but as the
blessed do in heaven, rejoice in the happiness
and glory of others as if it were their own,
be proud of their priests, thank God for them,
cherish them, provide for them ?

And we must be pardoned a word here.
We must ask to be forgiven when we venture

to remark that many Catholics in this Christian country have not the faith of the poor savages abroad who have been taught the truths of religion. These poor untutored people, savages no longer, instinctively feel with the apostle that " they who preach the Gospel should live by the Gospel." They take the young missionary under their care, looking to his wants, his food, &c., providing his lodging and the rest, in the best way they can, and certainly the privations he may have to endure arise not from want of thought on the part of his poor flock, or from an unwillingness to deprive themselves for his sake, for they do that: they will bring him food regularly, and however little it may be to his taste, it will be the best they have. They think themselves responsible to God for the care of the priest He has sent to them with such beautiful news about Himself, and not only news, but who has the power to bring Him to them, to give Him to them, that they may live no longer the natural, the sinful, the miserable lives they had led, but lives of supernatural peace and joy. They reverence the very hand of the priest, the hand that gives them the Bread of Life, the Heart's Blood of their Brother Jesus, who wished to make them one with Himself. These unlearned savages are truly taught of God, and are an example to many Christians, who either from ignorance or supineness neglect their duty to their pastor, who hinder his work of good to souls, distracted and harassed as he is often obliged to be with " pounds, shillings, and pence," and indeed obliged at times to plead with his people for the very necessaries of life, and plead perhaps in vain. Such extreme cases, it is to be hoped, are rare, but they do occur, and at least it may be safely said that in every congregation there are some who may well learn a lesson from the savages in this respect. Then again have I known poor priests obliged to spend their valuable time, every moment of which they needed for their mission work, in writing begging letters which some of their people might well have written for them, necessary begging letters, if debts are to be paid, churches and schools to be built where they are absolutely needed. Pastor and people should be one; his anxieties should be their anxieties, his cares their cares. We must be pardoned this digression. I know it is not needed in many places, but in far too many it is.

If Mary's children will only live in union with their Mother, they will learn from her

Heart her love of priests: they will reverence them, they will support them, they will save them all the trouble they possibly can. Sweet Mother, we do love those whom you love, we do wish to do by them as you would have us do. We will ever see in our Lord's anointed priests His representatives, we will reverence and obey them as such, we will be what Mary would have us be, we are lovers of her Heart, we do love its loves, and we know that one of the great loves of Mary's Heart is her love of Christ's priests, those blessed ones of all most highly favoured on the earth, those too who have such a hard battle to fight in the Church Militant, those who are so set apart and separated from all for the love of their Lord. We will think of our Mother in heaven watching over, keeping and protecting her priests on earth. We will pray that many may consecrate themselves entirely to her as her own, that they may place themselves entirely at her disposal, so that she may use them at will, and that they may live but for her love, which will be the surest means of their being devoted entirely to the love of Jesus and of God.

That they may live to preach the love of Mary; live to give her more children; love to live that they may teach all minds to know,

all hearts to love her; love to live, since life
is sweet when " lived as Mary lived it;" love
to live to suffer for her Son, their Lord and
Master. Motherlike in his sufferings and
trials endured for his people is the true pastor;
motherlike in his forgetfulness of self, leading
two lives, one of exterior work, of solicitude
for his flock, another of interior love and care
for Jesus, and in this again is he so like Mary.
The priest is guardian of the Blessed Sacrament, as Mary was of the Infant Jesus. It is
more to him than his life, as Jesus was to
Mary. He is bound to protect it before his
life. God has confided the Word Incarnate to
His priest as He did to Mary. Our Lord's
consecrated spouses have their Love dwelling
under the same roof with them; they may
watch, adore, and bring Him flowers to adorn
His altar; they strive to make His home
with them a happy one, (to use our poor
human mode of expression,) but they are not
His guardians; the priest alone is our Lord's
guardian; he has charge and care of Jesus.
Is he not like Mary? Will we not, then,
look upon them as favourites of Mary, as
special children of hers, and will we not love
and honour them as such, and so prove ourselves truly Mary's own? Show that we
really live in her Heart and by it, that we

have renounced our own selves, our own loves, to live by Mary's loves, and then one day come to the heaven of love above, there to find that those who are nearest and dearest to the Heart of God are those who on earth were near and dear to the Heart of Mary.

---

## NINETEENTH DAY.

### The Love of our Lady for the Holy Mass.

Mary's love for the holy sacrifice of the New Law, the sacrifice of the spotless Lamb of God, the offering of the life of Jesus her own Son ! Yes, this is the Holy Sacrifice of the Mass, the offering of the Body and Blood of Jesus, Mary's Son. Wonderful thought ! Mystery full of wonders and beauties is the thought of Mary hearing Mass when on earth. Still more wonderful to meditate on Mary viewing from her bright throne in heaven the Masses ever being offered here on earth. We can only have some faint, some very distant idea of the joy, the adoration, the extatic love with which it inspired and still inspires her. But Mary's children must in their measure participate in her joy in the offering of this adorable sacrifice. When she was present at

Holy Mass on earth, what must have been the feelings of that Mother's Heart. We may well ask what must they have been, but to answer is not so easy. Would that we could assist at Mass as Mary did; would that we could enter a little into her feelings. Pray silently now, pray earnestly, come closer to your Mother, creep beneath her mantle, watch her assisting at Holy Mass. What are her thoughts? At least we may be sure that it brings back to her mind both Bethlehem and Calvary, both the birth of Jesus and His death. The priest is in her place now, holding the new-born Child. She thinks of her joy as He lay a little Infant in her arms, and she pressed Him to her breast. Again she views the sacrifice of Calvary renewed. The Blood of Jesus is offered to His Eternal Father in satisfaction for the sins of all mankind, pleading for mercy, imploring all graces, offering befitting worship to the Most High, thanking the Ever-blessed Trinity for the gifts bestowed upon mankind. It is for all these ends the Sacred Humanity of Jesus, His Precious Body and Blood is offered, and Mary enters fully, comprehensively into the wondrous mystery of divine love made manifest in this adorable sacrifice. It is Calvary again without its bitter pang; it is all joy to her now, pure joy, joy that would have sent the saints into ecstasy.

Oh, it was a fair sight in heaven to see Mary attending Mass on earth. All her virtues shone most brilliantly then, above all, her special, her favourite one, her humility. We indeed cannot enter into her dispositions, we can only try to form some faint conception of what they must have been. We could never hear Mass as Mary did; but why not try to do our best? Why not try to assist at Holy Mass with something at least of the same spirit as Mary? Why not pray that we may appreciate this adorable sacrifice, this marvellous mystery better? And why, why not attend daily Mass if we possibly can do so, if by a little self-sacrifice, by rising earlier, or by putting ourselves to some no very great inconvenience we can hear Mass more frequently than we do? Oh, why do we not do it? If you value your own soul, if you value the souls of others, if you value God Himself, go and attend at Mass. Attending at Mass is like being in the pool of Probatica at the time the healing waters were stirred by the angel of God. One greater than the angel descends to heal and strengthen the souls of men. Attending at Mass is the creature's best worship of the Creator. At Mass you can say to God with confidence that in the offering you make Him of the infinite merits of His Son, you have more than satisfied for the debt you owed Him. Will He not then, for the sake of what is over and above of those infinitely superabundant merits, give you all the graces for which you ask for yourself and others? Daily our wants and crosses increase; daily is the Mass offered, by assisting at which we shall obtain every grace we need, patience in our wants, resignation in our crosses, strength to resist temptations. Only let us assist at Mass as often as we can, and with the best devotion we can, and soon, very soon, will our lives show differently to those around us, soon will the saints in heaven be rejoicing in our true conversion and in our victories.

Daily the priest stands at God's altar offering the Adorable Sacrifice; and daily the angels gather around and wonder at the coldness of men, since so few besides themselves assist the priest at this most solemn, this most momentous act, the offering the "tremendous mysteries," which, if he fully realized as the angels realize it, were it not for the grace of his ordination, he would hardly be capable of offering. We read of St. Philip Neri saying Mass, and wonder not that he was seen floating in mid-air; we wonder not that the hours flew by, and he still standing entranced as it were at the altar.

Let us keep near to Mary during Mass, and she will show us how to gather grace most plentifully. She will fill us with her spirit, her spirit of joy, of delight, that God is thus adored on earth; that human nature offers worship to God infinitely greater than the angels of themselves ever have offered, or ever could. Sweet Mother of Jesus, on the altar we too will rejoice; we will be glad, we will attend at Mass in an unselfish, happy spirit, rejoicing that we are able thus to rejoice; rejoicing that, after having mourned for our own unworthiness, our incapability of worshipping our God as we should, we have the adorable Sacrifice of the Mass, and know that there is our worship, that there is our adoration, that there is our pure and perfect devotion to our great Creator.

Mary, thy own will never miss this opportunity of loving God, of offering Him their homage. Place us where we may daily assist at it; show us how we can best hear Mass, and obtain from it grace to live as thy own should in this world, their noviciate for the world to come.

Behold the pure oblation offered on this

earth "from the rising to the setting of the sun." Behold the Host in the hands of the priest; see, It is Mary's Son; It is the fruit of her womb, Jesus. From ten thousand altars on earth this Sacrifice is offered to heaven, and the justice of God is satisfied, His anger is appeased, His love satisfied, the fountains of His mercy opened, and the flood of Mary's joy overflows, for her sacrifice of her Son is continually giving new glory to her God, drawing down new graces upon the earth, the earth that was once her home, and on which she wishes again to live in the persons of her children.

---

## TWENTIETH DAY.

### The Love of our Lady for Holy Communion.

Never did saint thirst for Holy Communion as Mary did; no creature ever appreciated, ever understood this wonderful Sacrament as Mary has; no one's preparation for Communion ever came so near to be what it is befitting such preparation should be, as Mary's, and this because of the profound sense she had, that she, even she, the Immaculate one, was not worthy to receive her

6

God in this marvellous mystery of His love. It was because of this knowledge of her own nothingness before God, that Mary came so near being worthy; that she gave her God such delight, such joy, when she received Him in Holy Communion. What were her thoughts? what did she say to Him? how did she receive Him? Ah, sweet Mother, as we may in our measure receive Him too, if our faith were more lively; if we did but exercise our faith, hope, and love more earnestly; if we turned our thoughts more to God in the course of the day, and less to the things of the world; if we were not so engrossed with the petty affairs of life; if we were not so very much of this earth—so earthly. Mother, we see thee, as it were, opening thy breast at one time to receive Jesus again as thy own little Infant, at another as the Boy of Nazareth, whom thou used to fondle and caress; again as Jesus, Saviour of the world, walking amongst the sons of men, the most comely amongst them. Then would Mary press close to the Sacred Heart, that Heart she could not reach when He hung on the cross, and then would she remain in happy thanksgiving, with glad rapturous joy and delight that it is all over now, and that Jesus can suffer no more. She recollected the years of agony she passed in her anticipation of His agony; the moments laden with sorrow had passed one by one, each with its own separate burden of grief, for the sorrows, the sufferings of her Jesus. His Passion was vividly before her mind; not more plainly had the prophet seen the future Messiah, and described Him as a leper, and as one struck by God, than Mary saw Jesus in His coming Passion; even during His childhood, when she laid Him to rest, she saw Him rudely laid upon His cross, when she saw Him with outstretched arms running to embrace her, in spirit she beheld Him with arms stretched out upon the cross. Oh, that long living martyrdom of Mary! and now in her wonderful Communion she possesses Him in calm content and delight, for she knows He is in supreme felicity, in unspeakable joy,—she knows He can never suffer more. She was content; and why are we not more like Mary in her Communions? why are we not more content? We should not look for sensible devotion, for great spiritual consolation, but a certain quiet, calm content we ought to experience. Why do we not? Because we are so selfish; because we love Jesus so little. We are not thinking enough of Him, we are thinking too much about ourselves, hoping for some great spiritual consolation, half thinking perhaps (though we would not acknowledge it to ourselves) that we are favourites with Jesus, and that He will show us some special tokens of love, and so on.

Why do we not please Jesus more when we go to Holy Communion? Because we do not go as Mary did: and why do we not? because we are too bent upon pushing ourselves forward; we are thinking too much of ourselves. We are like rude ignorant people we sometimes meet who, having been invited out by those above them, instead of remembering their humbler position, and behaving as becomes them, expose their vulgarity by loud talking, assuming airs, and so on. Let us copy Mary, and learn from her how we should receive and entertain Jesus. Let us lose the thought of ourselves in Jesus. If we wish to make our Communions in the most perfect manner we can, let us draw Mary to our side, let us humble ourselves, let us forget ourselves; it is perhaps better than even thinking of our own unworthiness, to forget ourselves, to put ourselves on one side entirely, and to ask Mary to entertain Jesus for us. If we trust ourselves to our Mother, she

will make our Communions glorious to God,
pleasing to herself, and fruitful to us.

Mary, lover of the Precious Blood, will
teach us how to realize the value, how to
reverence, how to adore that Precious Blood
shed from the Wounds of Jesus on the cross,
which we then receive into our hearts. Good
God, we have almost envied the chalice as it
was held in the happy hands of the priest at
Mass, but in that supreme moment of communion we ourselves are chalices of the Precious Blood, looked upon with love and delight
by the Eternal Father, almost the envy of the
holy angels. It is the thought of the joy we
give to God, when Jesus is with us at that
time, when our Father in heaven looks down
upon us, and sees not us, but Jesus in us. It
is the thought that there is no act they can
perform which can give to God the glory that
we can give Him by the adorable sacrifice and
holy communion, which may well, I say, make
the angels envy us. It is the knowledge of
the grace and strength they there receive
which makes holy souls run to communion.
Let us, then, hasten to holy communion, too;
let us remember that having given all we
have, ourselves, our merits, our good works, to
our Lady's keeping and disposal, we must try
to increase our gift, and by going to holy

communion we can best do this. Let us
remember we are not our own, we are our
Lady's own; we must use ourselves as her
property, her possession.

Sweet Mother, prepare us thyself for holy
communion, by obtaining for us the fitting
dispositions, and we will resolve for thy sake,
that as often as we are allowed to do so, so
often will we approach this heavenly banquet,
and thus please thee, our Mother. We have
given thee ourselves; we will give thee,
together with ourselves, our Jesus.

---

## TWENTY-FIRST DAY.

### The Love of our Lady for our dear Lord's Spouses.

The Mother's love for the spouses of her
Son. Must not this be a very special love, a
love with a very distinct character of its own.
The love of the Queen of Heaven for those who
are to "follow the Lamb whithersoever He
goeth," those who are the most precious fruits
of Jesus's Passion, the lilies of this vale of
tears. Yes, most surely, for the true spouse
of Jesus crucified in body and soul with her

Lord a wondrous love fills the Mother's
Heart. With what love does not she in
heaven watch over Jesus's spouses on earth;
with what tender care, with what solicitude,
that they be not tarnished by the world's sin;
what difficulties does she not remove from
their path; what obstacles does she not enable
them to surmount; how carefully does she
not prepare these her favoured children for
their espousals with Jesus; how zealous is
she that they be properly arrayed; how
thoughtfully does she, their Mother in heaven,
do her part, do all in her power, if they but do
their part, if they do what lies in their power.

Happy souls whom Jesus calls to union
with Himself, and who come readily to His
call; but sad indeed is it for those whom He
calls and who do not come. To those who are
docile to the voice of Jesus, to those who,
acknowledging their unworthiness, come almost shrinkingly to His feet, and kneeling
there, ask only that they may fulfil His will,
still longing to yield to love's invitation, and
to unite their souls indissolubly with their
God-Lover; to those who long for this, and
yet turn from themselves with loathing and
disgust as they think of their utter unworthiness of this great dignity, recognizing too
well their own vileness and baseness, and who

truly appreciate the dignity, the greatness, of
the title of spouse of Jesus, a title angels
might envy; to those who under obedience
enter upon this state, and who ever remember
what they are in God's sight; to such as
these, I say, Jesus stretches out His arms,
and draws them to Himself upon the cross.
Oh, that embrace of Jesus crucified! Would
that the world knew what it is like. Mary,
sweet Mother, fair flower of the earth, is it
not thy own who are most perfectly prepared
to be the spouses of Jesus? Is it not those
who have clung to thee even when—shall we
say it?—thou didst seem a hard Mother?
Thy mortifications were so bitter, the cleansing, purifying process seemed so severe, almost
too much for poor human nature, which at
times was forced to cry out in its agony. But,
Mother, thou didst know what was best for
us; thou didst lay us on the rack; thou didst
melt away self-love in the crucible of severe
suffering. It was well; we know it now, as we
look from our cross upon the world, as we rest
in the arms of Jesus, and find peace even in
this world on His Sacred Human Heart,
Human although the Heart of God.

We no longer live, but Jesus lives in us;
He loves us, we are wholly His, and the
Mother of fair love watches with intense solici-

tude that we remain ever thus aloof from all
other loves, with no other love but the love of
Jesus, loving all else in Him, with Him, and
for Him.   She assists the soul thus linked to
Jesus, she helps it in every way, she aids it
most powerfully, or it could not remain so
pure, so chaste, so entirely detached from the
things of this world, as a spouse of Jesus
should be.   The souls of Mary's own are dear
to Jesus, they are indeed His own.   Our Lady
does not allow those who trust to her care to
become the brides of Jesus without having
wherewithal to meet their Lord and Love, so
as to please Him.   She clothes them in the
nuptial robe; she takes a pride, to speak in
human fashion, in adorning her docile children, those who place themselves submissively
in her hands; and she strengthens their souls,
that they may be firm in their allegiance to
Jesus their true Love; and she watches with
ineffable delight the transformation of their
souls, the wonderful union with the sacred
soul of Jesus, the likeness that takes place,
the gradual growth of grace, the liquefying
effect of love, the marvellous constant communion.   This sweet Mother watches all, sees
all, with wondrous joy; she sees more than
the soul itself can see, for the soul is scarce

conscious of the operations of grace within it, but Mary is.

The soul, however, certainly does feel itself sweetly encompassed with the grace of God; it feels that it is steadily advancing towards Him; it feels the desire to please Him growing greater, and it feels at the same time the hatred of its own sinful self growing greater too; it could not bear the sight of itself in God's pure sight, but that the brightness of light from God's great life makes its own little life to be lost, forgotten, just when the view of itself without the grace of God would be too much.   Oh God, these souls to Thee are precious, priceless.   Would there were more. There are many such in name, and, thank God, there are many spouses of Jesus who are not so in name, but they are so in reality, for He is all theirs, and they are all His.   Then thank Him, you who live in religion, His consecrated spouses; but remember much will be expected of you; remember that you must bring Him interest for the talents given you; you must be fruitful spouses of Jesus; you must not be sterile, barren; you must bring Him souls; whether in an active or a contemplative order, you have to help Him each in your own way in His great work of saving souls. Thank Him your Lord, you who are His

consecrated spouses in religion; but thank
Him likewise, you who are His own in the
world, for you are as lights to Jesus in a dark
and sin-stained world; you are bright spots,
well pleasing in His sight. Persevere in
your difficult path; be not disheartened; you
may not seem to do the good you would; but
cling close to Mary; push on through the
perils by which you are surrounded; that
bright star of the sea will beam brightly upon
you. Look up; Mary is beckoning you
onward; the longest life is so short, your
journey will soon be ended. Jesus your
Spouse is awaiting you; He is longing to
comfort His own; the day is not far off when
you will meet Him your Love. How gladly
will you look into His face, how will your
soul spring towards Him. What will He say
to you? What are the first words you will
speak to Him?

Oh, ineffable union, secret known to God
alone, the first communion in the world to
come, the first and never-ending communion
between Jesus and His spouse; that union
which, begun in time, is cemented in the
never-ending ages of eternity; that first
greeting of Jesus in heaven with His beloved
one from earth, will ever continue in its first
freshness, when the day of doom has passed,

when this world has no longer " this generation," which has passed away for ever. There
in peace, in extatic love and joy, rests, in
the arms of Jesus, His earthly spouse, His
favoured one, whom He called, whom He
loved in the land of hope, who listened, loved,
answered, and now receives the reward of the
hope practised so well in the struggles and
trials of this life, which is not wearisome to
those who love, but is sweet, with a slight
foretaste of the sweetness of the life to come.

---

## TWENTY-SECOND DAY.

### The Love of our Lady for those aiming at Perfection.

Those who are aiming at perfection are
truly Mary's own; those who have resolved to
live perfect lives, or at least to be aiming at
it, are truly hers; and well does their Mother
assist them. When she sees it is no passing
thought, no fancy, but a real, deep, earnest,
working resolution to do ever what is most
perfect, to live but to please God, then, when
her child sets to work in earnest, does the
sweet Mother above all mothers set to work

too. People grow down-hearted about aiming at perfection; the lives of the saints seem so far above them. But they know not the help God gives to those who are really in earnest, to those who He sees will not abuse His graces. It may seem a strange thing to say, but nevertheless we think it true, that the life of a saint, the life *all* for God, is in reality easier, with all its trials, sufferings, and sorrows, than the life which is only half for God. Really plunge into the most perfect life, under wise direction, and with all prudence, and then will be found the hidden sweetness there is in it; then we shall know that we have seen but the exterior life of the saints, and knew not how sweet the Lord is to those who truly love Him and serve Him with their whole hearts.

We have spoken of our Lady's love for saints. We have said that one saint gives more glory to God than a whole nation of ordinary Christians. But we are told that this applies not alone to the saints, but also to those who are striving to be saints, who are really aiming at perfection. They are most dear to the Heart of God, most dear to the Mother's Heart. They are watched over in their strugglings, they are loved in their trials, they are supported in their tempta-

tions, they are prayed for by Mary with unwearied earnestness. Oh, then, let us give
joy to our Mother's Heart by an earnest, firm
resolution to be what she so wishes us to be,
perfect in word and work. Let us now consider how we are to set about it.

"What more could I do for My vineyard
that I have not done?" In the first place we
must all of us from time to time go aside
quietly, and reflect upon our office, our charge,
our state of life, the particular work appointed
us. We must look upon that, whatever it is,
as the portion of our dear Lord's vineyard
which He has committed in a great measure
to our care, which He has put into our unworthy hands. "What more could I do for
My vineyard that I have not done?" You
must repeat the words slowly, thoughtfully,
prayerfully, and if a prayer is sent from the
heart, a sincere, earnest, humble prayer, light
from God will certainly come, and it will
reveal to you much which before was hidden.
Thanks to His goodness and mercy, it may
not perhaps reveal many sins of commission;
but the sins of omission, how many, how
various, how repeated. If we do not see them
it is because we have not light; if we are
going on in a quiet, self-satisfied, complacent
way, we are not living in the sunshine of God's

Holy Spirit. We are wrapt up in our own dark spirit, and see not ourselves as we really are in the sight of God ; and as those do see who are leaning upon God, constantly recurring to Him and consulting Him, taking every opportunity they can of turning to Him, availing themselves of quiet times now and then afforded them, an illness for instance, or indisposition, or a journey, or any other occasion which makes a break in the ordinary routine of their lives, as a means of holding closer communion with God, of consulting Him, of reviewing the past, and seeing how they have served Him. At such times a clearer view of things rises in the mind ; we think of what we have done, and see more distinctly what we might have done, and ought to have done, and what we have left undone. When this is the case let us not be discouraged, let us not lose heart, but let us thank God with a grateful heart for the light He has given us. Let us humble ourselves, and acknowledge our unworthiness to hold the office, to occupy the position that we do, whatever it may be. Let us acknowledge that, being so little, so worthless, God chose us that He might show His power in us, that so no flesh might glory in His sight. Let us, then, tranquilly acknowledging the mistakes, the omissions, that

we have been guilty of, almost rejoice that
we have seen and understood a little more of
our own nothingness, rejoice in our own little-
ness, since it will all be for God's greater
glory, whose power will be exalted in our
weakness, and then seek to discover the root,
that is the causes of our failures and mistakes,
of whatever kind they may have been, and
then turn to God with earnest prayer, that we
may obtain the grace to do better for the
future. Dear God, how we advance in His
love by our failures, when we are humble
enough to acknowledge them, and own them to
ourselves. What a pity we do not. God
help us! how impregnated are we with the
poison, the nastiness, if I may be allowed the
word, of self-love. We ought not to wonder
that we have made mistakes, we ought rather
to wonder that we have not had some grievous
fall, we ought to be thankful we have not
grown deliberately careless and negligent in
our duties. There is danger of that, but not
so much in Mary's own as in others. Their
Mother has taught her children not to indulge
their feelings, not to be actuated by caprice or
mere natural inclination. She has taught
them that sentiment is not religion, she has
taught them in various ways the grand lesson
of detachment, so that they commence their

work in a spirit of union with God, and a work of importance in the same spirit as one of less consequence. They commence it and they continue it to fulfil the will of God, and consequently there is little perhaps of that feverish fervour at the beginning, which soon dies out; but there is no diminution of earnestness in their work, and a growing desire to do it well, and a constant increase in the perfection with which they perform it, often looking back to see how they might have done better, and what they have left undone, and thus they will be daily advancing in the path of virtue. Who cannot see the mistakes they have made in the month just past, the want of perfection interiorly and exteriorly in their daily life? No one, but the one who is not making nor trying to make any progress. Such persons indeed do not see their mistakes, do not see their omissions, do not see sometimes their falls. They are blinded by self. May God preserve us from this blindness; may God preserve us from the misery of not perceiving the failures, the faults of the past. Let us not encourage that self-deception, that self-love, which strives to hide from itself the mistakes made, which will not look them in the face, which glosses them over even when a light from God, a whisper from our guardian angel, would show us ourselves in a somewhat truer light. A truly humble person is glad to avail himself of anything that will make him more humble. Humility strives to exaggerate, if possible, its defects, not with a false exaggeration, but in order to be truthful, knowing, as humble souls do, (for humble souls have light, or they could not be humble,) that it is easy indeed to deceive oneself, and seeing, for they cannot help seeing, that others deceive themselves, they think it but natural that they too may do so. When we speak of "false exaggeration," we mean, for instance, such cases as persons saying they are very wicked, that such-and-such calamities have befallen them on account of their sins, and so on, and then, when told of some fault, and no very great one either, they immediately excuse themselves, and will not see themselves as others do to whom their blindness to their imperfections is very evident, and who in charity would be glad to help them to correct themselves by making them see themselves in a truer light. We know we have to cast first the beam out of our own eye if we would see to cast out the mote out of our brother's eye. Still, fraternal correction is a duty at times, but a duty very difficult to perform properly and wisely, and not to be attempted unless after much prayer and self-humiliation in the sight of God. And indeed it is a hard and thankless task to strive to show those who are thus shut up in their own esteem how others see them, to show them a little more clearly how God looks upon them. It is a hard task, and often apparently a hopeless one. If the truth is clearly brought home to them, they will sometimes begin to take a despairing view of themselves, or it will rouse the spirit of pride and presumption that is in them, and leave them worse than they were before.

Well now, in times of retreat, or other times set apart for serious thought, which are so necessary for all, let us set out with the strong conviction that in looking either into ourselves and our duty to ourselves, or in examining how we have performed the special duties of the state in which God has placed us, there are many faults that we do not yet see, but which we must strive to discover, many commissions, many, very many omissions, a vast number of mistakes, and that it will be well, not only for our greater humiliation, but for our greater happiness both here and hereafter, that we should see. How many times have we decided a matter without any recourse to the Father of Lights for direction? How many things have we done in word and

deed directly contrary to the will of our sweet
Jesus? done them, perhaps, in ignorance, but
it should humble us to know that if we were
living in closer union with God we should not
make such mistakes. We should not be discouraged when we discover much that we
have done amiss; on the contrary, we should
be glad, because it is a sign we are making
progress. The first step in improvement is to
know what has to be improved, and for this
we must look back over the road we have
travelled, see the wrong steps we took, see
what difficulties and hindrances we could have
avoided. It is folly to learn nothing from the
past, whether regarding the conduct of our own
soul, or the discharge of our particular office
and work. It is indeed in regard of our
special charge, the particular duties of our
state of life, that I am now speaking, for in the
manner we perform these lies our perfection.
No matter how small a charge it may be, no
matter how seemingly unimportant the duties
of our daily life, they are certainly a work
God has given us to do; they have to be
done for Him, and not for creatures; "not
serving to the eye as pleasing men, but as
pleasing God." Now let us examine how we
have performed these duties. What was our
interior intention? Are our motives perfectly

pure? Have we been impatient with those
under us? Have we been overbearing?
Have we been unlike our gentle Jesus? Have
we been negligent, untidy, disorderly? Have
we wasted precious time? Have we been
anxious to perform our work well simply that
we might get praised for it? Have we let
vain-glory creep in? Alas, how fresh questions
keep springing up. Let us sit quietly in
God's presence, and consider all we have done,
and how we have done it. Have we behaved
to the poor, to the sick, as we would to our
dear Lord? Have we been earnest about
their souls? When we have thought of all
this, when we have reflected again and again
upon the words, " What more could I do for
My vineyard that I have not done?" When we
·have, in short, thoroughly examined ourselves
upon our positive duties, we will think of one
thing more we may do for God, which will
liken us indeed to the blessed above. This,
however, must be the subject of a separate,
serious, nay, solemn consideration, for it may
be the very rubicon, the passing of which may
ensure our living henceforth as God's hidden
saints on earth, and therefore hereafter as
God's glorious saints in heaven.

# TWENTY-THIRD DAY.

## The Love of our Lady for those aiming at Perfection.—Continued.

[This Conference or Consideration was, as will be perceived, addressed to religious, but is given here, as it may be not without profit to those who are aiming at perfection in the world.]

We are to continue to-day our thought of the love of our Lady's Heart for those aiming at perfection. We have already seen that our perfection lies in the perfect performance of our daily duties, and this leads us to consider something further we may do, which will greatly please our Mother, and yet it is something we hardly like to mention, it may be such a new thought to some, and may startle them as being quite beyond their power; but we need not be alarmed, it is something not to be done all at once. Let us look upon it as something which perhaps years hence we may succeed in, but still which there is no reason why we should not try even now to practise in a small way, training ourselves to it by degrees. It is one thing more we may do for God; the one thing

that will make us resemble the blessed in
heaven; the one thing that really enables us
to put in practice our dear Lord's prayer,
"Thy will be done on earth as it is in heaven;"
it is the one thing more that will endear us
greatly to our heavenly Mother, that will
make her Heart burn with a singular love for
us as from her home above she sees her children really striving to do on earth as the
blessed do in heaven.

"Thy will be done on earth as it is in heaven." "Be ye perfect, as your Heavenly
Father is perfect." They are our dear Lord's
words. He wishes us to be perfect. "If thou
wilt be perfect," again He speaks, "be ye holy
as I your God am holy," which was said even
in the Old Law to those who had not the helps
to be perfect that we have now. Then shall we
not really strive in thought, word, and work
to be perfect? Oh, the happiness, the liberty,
the joy of spirit they possess who are really
striving to be perfect. There are some who
have made a vow to do always what is most
perfect, and it is this I am now speaking of as
the one thing more you can do for God. Now
far be it from me to wish you to do that at
once and now, but what I wish is that you
should look forward to it, that you should
regard it as something not at all beyond the

reach of any Christian, thus to draw still closer to God by this holy, happy vow, which will so liken you to the blessed spirits above. And therefore I should indeed be glad if on the day of your profession you would make a strong resolution that you will begin to strive to do ever what is most perfect, and in the examination of your conscience to ask yourselves how you have kept that resolution. Remember, your resolution is not a vow, there is no question of sin even supposing you do not always keep your resolution. To explain my meaning; suppose you have a doubt what is best to do where duty or obedience do not clearly settle the matter for you; for instance, shall I now go to confession or not? shall I say this or keep silent? shall I do this that I am about in this way or in that way? Well, you say, I intend and have resolved to do what is best, and this and not that seems to me the best. Even should you make a mistake, and find out that what you thought was best is not so, it is no manner of consequence, you *intended* to do the best, and that is all you need be concerned about. Matters of consequence as a rule are not doubtful, duty clearly points the way, and then all that concerns your resolution is to do them in the best way you can.

What I am recommending may be thought

to engender a feeling of bondage; and yet those who are most bound even by vow will tell you that they enjoy the greatest liberty. Take the soul that is bound to obedience, poverty, and chastity; take the happy spouse of Christ, look in her face, does she seem as if she were living under any uncomfortable yoke? See again the cheerless, clouded, often gloomy face of one who is subject to her passions; she has made no vows to God, she is not bound to Him in any special manner: no, she is more bound to her own passions, and there is no slavery like that. Indeed it is a hard bondage, the bondage to one's own will, to one's own inclinations, which tyrannize over the best desires and aspirations of the soul. No one knows, no one can know, but those who have experience of it, what liberty, what freedom of soul is produced by religious vows and the faithful practice of these vows, which bind to a certain course of action, a certain line of conduct; and that course of action, that line of conduct in harmony with the will of God. Let us try to bring the thought more home to us, in order that we may be more grateful to God for the grace He has given us to enable us thus to give to Him that which is most acceptable to Him, our own wills. Think of a soul which feels the call from God to conse-

7

crate itself to Him, and yet hesitating, trembling, fearing to do so, hesitating from love of creatures, love of the world, hesitating to make the sacrifice, trembling lest it should not be able to fulfil it, fearing it will be more than it can do, and yet trembling lest it should be resisting the grace of God. It looks forward to years of subjection, years of hardship, years spent in subduing self, years, as it fancies, of wearisome struggle. It sees so much that is really true, and yet so much also that is untrue, since there is so much that it does not see. It does not see the joy, the liberty springing from this voluntary bondage. The blessed are blessedly bound in heaven, and some foretaste of this bliss is the portion of many who, after having struggled with self, have bound themselves by vows to God. There is then no doubt or uncertainty, shall I do this or shall I not? shall I indulge these thoughts or shall I not? (I am not speaking, of course, of positively sinful thoughts, but of such as are useless, idle, or desponding.) Then comes to the mind the whisper, "I have resolved, or I have *vowed* to do ever what is most perfect, therefore I cannot do this action, I cannot think this thought." Happy the soul that lives ever in this state. Would there were more such; but, thank God, there have been many holy ones, living too in the world, in the midst of ordinary every-day duties, who have made this vow quietly and secretly. They have lived upon that vow, they have died in the fulfilment of it, and no one, but Almighty God and their confessor, has known the perfection these souls had arrived at. The very perfection of such souls hides itself and prevents its being particularly observed by others, for there was nothing overstrained, nothing peculiar or particularly noticeable about it. Though necessarily there would be a difference in conduct from that of an ordinary Christian, and this difference might sometimes cause umbrage and remark from others who do not pretend to be aiming at perfection, still these holy souls so avoid excess, are so simple, and devotion sits so happily upon them, that they often pass unobserved by those around, though not unobserved by the inhabitants of the other world, not unobserved by angels and saints, but noticed and blessed by them; not unobserved either by evil spirits, who rage incensed as they see the good done by them, and discover to their chagrin how these pure and holy souls baffle all their attempts to lead them astray, and likewise hinder their malicious attempts in regard of others.

Shall we not join their number, shall we not look forward in course of time to making ourselves nearer and dearer to our Lord by this final vow ?  Begin now to be perfect in thought, word, and work ; begin now to fight against all imperfections ; make a resolution, first a simple one, such as we make at our meditations ; then a more solemn one, but still one which, even if you break it, of itself involves no sin ; then go on, it may be with many relaxations, many drawbacks, but still ever rising again, and encouraging yourself with the thought of the intense pleasure you will give to our good God by the solemn binding of yourself by vow, the relinquishing of yourself to Him which you hope one day to accomplish.  Go on thus, it may be, for many years, and at last some feast-day will come, a real festival for you, when your director will give you permission to complete your gift to God by this solemn, happy vow.  Then indeed will your life give great glory to God; then indeed will you, though bound so strongly, live in a delightful liberty, a life more resembling the life of the blessed above than a life led here on this sinful earth, which we nevertheless shall render less sinful than it was when we have made this vow.

Each in our own sphere, we might hinder

sin if we would ; we may at least in our own persons reduce the number of sinners, and if indeed we live in very sinful times and places, we must draw good from the evil by strengthening our souls, by purifying them by the sorrow and contrition these sins we see around us cause. Again we must repeat the saying of saints, that one saint is more to God, and does more for God, than a whole nation of ordinary Christians. Then do let us be saints ; the fulfilling of this vow that I have spoken of would make us such, would extend God's kingdom on earth, and reduce the kingdom Satan has set up in opposition to the good Lord and Creator of all things, our own Lord, our own sweet Jesus, whose we are even now, if faithful, His for ever, for endless ages on ages. Amen.

The vow I have been so strongly recommending would, of course, bind under sin, and sin would be committed if the person who has made it does with full deliberation what they know to be not the most perfect thing to do. The vow is simply to do at any moment what the soul believes to be most perfect. It necessarily implies consideration and prayer to know what is most perfect in thought, word, and deed, and constant examination as to the advance made in perfection as regards

charity, humility, and all the other virtues;
but the vow is not broken unless the soul
deliberately hesitates as to what is most perfect, and then decides and chooses to do what
it considers *not* the most perfect thing to do.
We need hardly remark that it might very
well happen that what the soul thought was
the most perfect thing might really not be so.
The vow, of course, would not be broken in
that case, the soul having the vow being to do
only what *seemed* the most perfect thing.

This is of the utmost importance to be re-
membered, in order to avoid anxiety and
scrupulosity. Remember then, that, as I said
before, you need not fear committing sin unless you deliberately choose what at the
moment you know or think to be the less
perfect course. .In by far the greater part of
your daily actions you will have no occasion
at all to deliberate, your course will be clearly
seen, duty and obedience will show you at
once what you have to do. And when duty
and obedience do not plainly point the way, it
is your will, your desire and intention, which
is all that you need attend to; even if by
mistake you do what is not so perfect, you
need have no concern, you will please God all
the same. The vow may be made in any form
or in any manner, to their director, before the

Blessed Sacrament or the statue of our Lady, after communion or at Benediction, with the lips, in a set form, or simply in the heart. The following form might be used, though another might do equally well :

I, N., child of Mary, who have consecrated myself entirely to her as her very own, to be wholly hers as Jesus was, do promise and vow that for the remainder of my life I will ever aim at what is most perfect in thought, word, and deed, that in every moment of my life what seems to me the most perfect thing to do that I will do, by the grace of God and with the help of His Holy Spirit, who, as I trust, has inspired, in answer to my prayer, to make this my vow to my Lord and God. Help me, holy angels, who bear witness to this my offering to my God. Help me, all ye holy saints, my patrons, friends of Him to whom I make my gift. Help me, Mary my most dear Mother, whose I am for time and eternity. Ye are the witnesses of this my vow; sustain me, that I hold fast to my present purpose, and that I may persevere to the end, until I come to the land where the perfect dwell in peace.

We need scarcely remark again that this
vow must not be made without leave from the
director; all should know they may not make
a vow, even so much as to say a Hail Mary
every day, without permission from their
director. And as regards this vow, no one
should even think of asking permission to
make it until they have *practised* it for
many years. A simple resolution to that
effect may be made with leave from the
director, a resolution not binding under sin.
It might be thought unnecessary to make
this remark, but there is a great deal of
ignorance about things that every one should
know, and people sometimes entangle themselves in many difficulties in their spiritual
life for want of acting under obedience to a
wise director. They wish to scale the mountain of perfection by some path of their own,
but it will only end in disaster. They sometimes begin entirely at the wrong end, like
people who should fancy they could build the
walls and put on the roof of a house before
they have made the foundation; this leads to
difficulties not easy to remedy. We do not
mean by this that people are to be always
teazing their confessors, wasting their valuable
time, and so on, as is the custom with certain

persons more pious than wise.* No, we do not mean this, but simply that each step we take in the spiritual life should be with the knowledge and approval of our director. This can be done in a few words; if we think before our Lord what it is we have to say, dot it down in our memory, or on paper, that we may remember it better. Do not suppose that I am advising you to keep a sort of spiritual diary, and get your minds engrossed with your own feelings and imaginations, which would be the case if you adopted such a pernicious practice; but I suggest writing as an occasional help, that you may be able simply and in a few words to say clearly what you think necessary

* This is a trial permitted by Providence to befall poor priests. There is generally one such person at least in most churches, as was remarked by a priest of his own congregation with some amount of satire, when he said that "God is merciful, and only allowed him *one*, for if there had been more he could not have borne it." It was suggested to another priest, after a certain lady's confession was finished, which had lasted—how long we will not say,—that he should quietly remark on the next occasion, "My child, you have forgotten one thing, you have forgotten to confess how much time you have wasted yourself, and how much of my time you have wasted, not to speak of the loss of time and the impatience you have occasioned to those who have been waiting in the church till you had finished."

to be said, and thus save your director both
time and trouble. In whatever you do in this
way let your sole motive be to fulfil the will
of God. In many it is a gratification, and
tickles their vanity to hear themselves talk,
and to think they have expressed themselves
well. With you, on the contrary, let it be for
the glory of God and the good of your own
soul. Mary's children should be scrupulous
about taking up the time of those to whom
time is so precious, to whom time means
saving souls, as with a devoted priest it really
does mean. We must be pardoned for finish-
ing our conference with this digression. What
has been said is not with any desire to find
fault, and we trust it will be taken in good
part by those to whom it applies. Even a
St. Francis Xavier could complain of women's
long conversations with their confessor, and (it
is a sister who writes this,*) the thoughtless
and needless way in which they take up the
time of those who direct them : and this valuable time is spent with perhaps little or no
profit, which might have been devoted to
God's glory in so many ways.

* Remark of reviser.

## TWENTY-FOURTH DAY.

### The Love of the Heart of our Lady for Domestic Life.

We do not think enough of this love of Mary for simple domestic life, indeed we often forget it entirely. And yet it is one of the most beautiful traits in her character; it seems the very essence of Mary, so to speak, to be simple, to perform the common ordinary duties of a wife and a mother, and to love them. Her Heart ever craved after one thing, namely, to walk simply before God and to be perfect, whatever might be the circumstances or condition of her life. But He gave her what her Heart most desired, the simple ordinary life of women, that she might live this life in her sweet, simple way, and sanctify it for the multitude of women who should follow her, that she might leave an example to her children, so sweet, so captivating, that they hereafter might love to walk in her footsteps; that she might be the pattern of a perfect woman to them. And such indeed she is, and so sweet is her example, that the world seems made holier, purer, by the very

name of Mary. Every good Catholic household seems penetrated with her influence, and
perfumed by her presence. Her statues and
pictures are everywhere, and everywhere remind us of herself, the pure simple Mary, the
holy woman, the gentle Virgin, the Mother
above all mothers. But she ever comes before
us in her own simplicity, that simplicity of
Mary which is unlike anything else. There
is nothing extraordinary about her in her outward conduct and demeanour, nothing exces-
sive, nothing exaggerated. She is a pure true
woman, lovely beyond conception; she is
*Mary*, unlike aught but herself. But for all
that, holy Mother, we wish to be like thee, as
far as we may; we wish to imitate thee; we
will follow thee in the way thou hast shown
us; our lives shall be in conformity to thine,
so far as our weakness will permit. If thou
hadst done extraordinary things we might still
have looked up to thee, longed to imitate thee,
and should not have been able; but thou hast
lived upon this earth as other women live,
working no miracles, doing nothing marvellous,
but for the greater part in the simple discharge of the duties of a quiet peaceful home,
only so perfectly, with such exquisite purity
of intention, with such ardent charity. We,
too, desire to live as thou hast done; thou

wilt surely help thy children, tender Mother
that thou art.

Mary is great as the Immaculate Virgin,
she is great as the marvellous Mother of God,
she is great as she stands on Calvary, offering
the greatest sacrifice ever creature offered to
God, of what was its own, for Jesus was hers,
He was her Son. Mary is great as Queen of
Heaven, but Mary is equally great in the
eyes of God in the simple actions of her daily
life, since in them she did God's will as perfectly as she did when she consented to become
His Mother. We love Thee, Mary, as we
watch thee, so quiet, so humble, performing
thy daily round of duties. Each action was an
offering, a gift, well pleasing to, the Most
High; each action was performed carefully,
earnestly, as though it were an act of religious
worship, and so indeed it was in Mary's eyes.
Mary sanctified the daily acts of life, and in
this her children can and must follow her
example. God is everywhere. He is adorable
everywhere. He should be adored everywhere. We work in His presence always.
It is with this thought ever in our minds that
we should work. It will not then matter to
us what our work is; the smallest action will
be performed as carefully as the greatest, and
our life will be beautiful in the sight of God.

Yes; it is not always what appear to us to be grand actions that are grand in the sight of God. They are indeed grand when performed purely for the love of God; but these same heroic actions may be done from unworthy, selfish, interested motives, and not be so pleasing to God as some most common-place, every-day actions proceeding from a purer motive. Who can understand the joy of God in His saints, whose days are full of such noble actions as these? We, too, naturally admire what is heroic and noble. See the applause that Grace Darling won for her one brave act in saving the lives of the poor shipwrecked sailors: but that may have been no more pleasing in the sight of God than the simple daily actions of many a chosen soul, both in the world and in the cloister, dear to the Heart of God, "for man seeth those things that appear, but the Lord beholdeth the heart." If we could see our lives as those in heaven see them; if we could but see how beautiful to the angels and saints the lives appear of those who on earth are " all for God," how differently should we feel, how differently should we act.

Do we think as we should of the quiet, simple life of Mary, full of its every-day ordinary actions? We have read of the saint who saw how a poor labourer was adding to his merit and his future crown in heaven by every brick he laid. Then what must Mary have done ? What was the purity of intention of that poor bricklayer laying his bricks compared to the intention with which Mary worked at her needlework, drew water from the well for her little household, cleaned the house and its humble furniture, and did all that was necessary for the simple poor cottage at Nazareth. The angels never tired of gazing at their Queen as she went from one duty to the other in the simple routine of her life. She grew more and more wonderful to them, and they loved human life, seeing it such as they had ne'er before seen it, "life as Mary lived it." Let Mary's children resolve to imitate their Mother; let them, wherever they may be, whether in the world or the cloister, resolve to imitate Mary by their cheerful, careful performance of their daily duties. Our Mother is looking lovingly upon us. Let us think of her sweet smiling face; let us earn from her the crown she is holding for us, which she is so anxious to bestow upon us, the reward the good God will give to all who are faithful to Him, and persevere in His service to the end. Let us never grow weary of our work; let us never grow remiss;

let us never yield to sloth. We shall not be
able to work for God in heaven, we shall rest
in Him there. Now is the time for toil and
labour. Now is the time to show our love for
God by fulfilling His will, which is that we
labour in the sweat of our brow in a spirit of
penance, though at the same time with a
spirit of joy that we are able thus to give gifts
to our God, the gift of ourselves and all our
faculties. Recollect that if the temptation of
sloth is given way to, there is an end to
sanctity for us. Recollect that if we begin to
perform our actions hurriedly, as matters of
slight import, we are in a state of delusion,
and our final perseverance in the right way is
doubtful. As a tree is known by its fruits, so
is the perfection of a soul known by its works,
it is the one true criterion. Watch how persons perform their work, and you will know
how near they are to God. You will know if
Jesus be dwelling as King within them or
not. One who works carelessly, who throws
things about untidily, who by thoughtless-
ness and carelessness creates disorder, that
soul is not living in close union with Jesus.
God is so orderly, so perfect, so beautifully
neat, if I may say so with reverence, in all
His ways. I cannot imagine such a thing as
an untidy or a slovenly saint, though in some,

doubtless, the poor body and its tidiness and cleanliness have been disregarded, but this was done from higher motives, and not from care-lessness or love of dirt for its own sake. If we are striving to make a home for Jesus in our hearts, to make His dwelling within us pleas-ing to Him, how carefully shall we work, how perfectly shall we strive to perform each action, with what a joyous, happy spirit, too. Not in a dull and slavish way; our service will not be a forced and oppressive, but a very cheerful, happy one; since all our actions will be offered to God, all our acts will be acts of love. We shall love our life of love and labour, and it is the Mother of fair love who will infuse this love into us, who will help her children to work in the same spirit as she did, who will send angels to assist them if they try to do their part, who will herself teach them the best way of performing their daily duties. Oh, lovely Mother, Queen of Angels, send thy holy angels to watch over thy chil-dren, and make them to live on earth as God's earthly angels, well pleasing in His sight and most dear to Him.

If Mary's children, then, would have their hearts in union with their Mother's Heart, they too must love domestic life, home life; they must consider home as their place of

work, and love it; they must think that their
principal work is to make home happy; they
must live in their household as Mary lived in
hers; they must put their heart in all they
do; they must make all their works acts of
love, as Mary did; and God will bless those
homes where the spirit of Mary thus lives.
May there be many such homes in this world,
that God may love it as in the beginning,
when He blessed it and pronounced it good.

---

## TWENTY-FIFTH DAY.

### The Love of our Lady for Infants.

Poor little ones, coming into this world, gifts
from God, every hour, indeed every moment
of the day and night, springing into existence.
It is of Mary's love for you we are now about
to speak.  Little souls, to whom God is every
instant imparting life, Mary loves you, for it
is by the almighty creating power of God that
you spring into life.  The good God's love is
continually satisfying its desire to give, and
He loves with an unspeakable love each new
life He gives, for it is His, and bears His own
image and likeness.  The Mother of fair love,
too, loves each little infant life, as it is given

to this world by God; intensely she loves it; she knows for what it is destined; she knows the throne it should have in heaven; she knows how precious that soul is to God; our Lady sees so much we do not see; she knows the love of the Sacred Heart for each individual soul that lives upon this earth; she knows and realizes,—oh, so differently from what we do, though we believe it,—she realizes, I say, how that Jesus shed His Blood for each and every soul upon this earth; the Heart of our Lady yearns over the infants that are daily born into the world; she wants these infants; she would have their souls washed and purified from sin as soon as they are born. She is truly Mother of all mankind, and would do a Mother's part by each, but she has to act by instruments: such is God's will; thus has God ordained, and so our dear Mother anxiously, wistfully looks for us to co-operate with her that the children daily born into the world may be baptized. This is a work we should pray about and use active exertions about, too; and yet how supine we are in a matter of such unspeakable moment. There are some who have prayed and laboured for this work, and how many little buds have they not laid at Mary's feet in heaven, to blossom for ever in the paradise of God; how many have they

not saved from the fearful calamity of dying
without baptism.

What a grand work it is, and we could do
it so easily. Look at St. Francis Xavier's
anxiety about this all-important matter.
See if one of the works he had most at heart
in the Indies was not the baptism of infants;
and let any one go up the courts and alleys of
our large towns, or into the cottages in our
villages, and they will quickly discover that
they need not go to heathen lands to be a St.
Francis Xavier. Poor little infants, they
daily die, and the Precious Blood is not poured
upon them, the Holy Ghost has not breathed
upon them, and by a little exertion we might
have saved them, we might have sent them to
heaven to adorn Mary's crown, with their
baptismal innocence upon them; but we
interested not ourselves in them. We cared
not to do the work ourselves, of visiting houses
and the cottages of the poor; and we cared not
to support the works of charity, to assist
charitable institutions, to help with our money
those religious and others who make it their
life to live for their neighbour, and who in
their errands of charity find how much more
might be done which cannot be done because
"the harvest indeed is ready, but the labourers

are few," and those few cannot do what they would for want of means.

Believe me, there is work to be done for Jesus that is not thought of. There are ways of saving souls, if we only wish to do so. Now what a great work, and what an easy one, is this for those who may not feel within them the power of converting souls, who have not the perseverance, the penance, the earnest trust, the never-failing hope which it requires. Here is easy work for you. Pray for infants, especially that they may have the grace of baptism. It is a most efficacious prayer. Infants have no will, no malice to resist or put obstacles in the way of prayer. When we pray for others, their perverse will may hinder the effect of our prayer, but with in‑ fants it cannot be so ; it is a kind of prayer most certain in its effect, a prayer the Mother's Heart in heaven will be most grateful for, a prayer that will bring untold blessings upon yourself, for the little ones will plead for you before the throne of God, when they are twined as a garland round Mary, giving her great joy and pleasure. Remember what a vast proportion of the human race die in in‑ fancy. Will they not plead for you on earth whom they so love, to whom they are so indebted, to whom they will be eternally

grateful? Yes, the ages will roll on, on,
on, and still the gratitude of these holy
innocents will be ever fresh, ever the same,
and they will be an eternal joy to you, an
eternal joy to the Mother-Heart of Mary, the
everlasting delight of God, the pure, fresh
blossoms of the Precious Blood.

Jesus, look with an eye of mercy upon all
the infants born into the world to-day. Remember how You suffered and died on Calvary
for them. Remember how Mary loves the
souls for whom You shed Your Precious Blood.
Think of the desire of her Maternal Heart,
that children who are born should be washed
in Thy Blood and born to a new life by baptism. Suffer not that these infants die without Thy grace. Bring to them the cleansing .
waters of baptism and save them.

Mother Mary, pray for thy children. Pray
that God may take to Himself to-day souls
now in His grace who to-morrow might sin.
Pray that children, now God's children, innocent, may die, (if it so please God, and He
foresees they would be eternally lost,) ere they
become His enemies by sin. O Mother of
Christians, Mother of mankind, since Jesus
was born and died for all mankind, pray for
all upon this earth that they may all indeed
be thine by being Christ's, that grace may be

brought to all, that none may die without baptism, and that those who have lost the innocence given them in baptism may be cleansed by contrition and penance ere they die.

Mother, inspire thy children to imitate thee, to live a life of devotion to others, a life of love for God and man. May none in God's Church stand idle all day, saying, " No man hath hired them ;" but send them, sweet Mother, into God's vineyard to work for the good Master who has promised to those who work a reward so great.

---

## TWENTY-SIXTH DAY.

### The Love of our Lady for the Dying.

The love of our Lady for the dying is the favourite thought of those who love her and are beloved by her, of those who have penetrated most deeply into the recesses of her loving Heart. The hour of death may be, and indeed is, in the offices of the saints, called the hour of birth. Mothers look forward to the hour of their children's birth, and then remember no more the anguish for joy that a child is born into the world. So it is with our Lady; she is full of loving solicitude when their

moment of death draws near, the precious
moment in which her children will be born to
a new and immortal life.  She looks for us to
help her in  their extremity; she looks for us
to assist her to bring her child to birth.
There on that bed of death lies the sufferer,
there lies the sinner, who has now but a small
portion of that time left wherein to gain eternal happiness; there lies the dying one in the
sight of the mother, the wreck and ruin of
what was once so beautiful, stricken  down
with mortal disease; angels of light and darkness hover near ; God is above, God is around,
God should be able to come now as a lover to
claim His own ; but it is not so, it cannot be;
besides mortal disease in the body, there is
mortal disease in the soul.  The disease of the
body is incurable; the soul can be cured;
well, well, the Mother knows it.  Who can
cure it ? who will cure it? what can cure it?
Love.  Yes; if we love one another we shall
cure one another's diseases, we shall heal one
another's infirmities, we shall help our Mother
in that moment when she will be so grateful
to us for help, that anxious moment, that all-
important moment, that time of trial.  If we
love the dying she will give us the oppor-
tunities to assist them, she will send her
angels to call those who she knows will help

her, whose love will give them power, whose faith and hope will enable them to work with her.

How callous, how cold we are. People may die; we care not. We may even visit death-beds, and human respect will hold us back from breathing even an act of contrition into the ear of the dying, or a loving thought of God, or the sweet name Jesus. We let them die, beautiful creatures of God, human beings like ourselves, we let them die uncared for, unthought of, lost perhaps, because not loved, and the Mother's Heart, when it inhabited a mortal body on earth, was pierced with unutterable sorrow at the sight of the lost children, grief greater than the united sorrow of the whole world was in that Mother-Heart of Mary at the thought of the many souls that would be lost through the callous indifference of those who professed to love her. Poor Mother, she mourned, yes, mourned as none other ever mourned, her Heart pierced with sorrow such as no other ever felt, save the Sacred Heart of Jesus. We will, as loving children, then, come to solace that Heart, come to draw from it grace to love others, grace to feel a little as Mary feels, grace to daily, hourly, pray for the dying, to help them as much as we can, and personally to

8

visit them when we can, and if hindered from
so doing by family duties, at least to assist
those who have given up home and family
that they may live in the homes of others,
nurse them in sickness, and do them all the
good they can, but who cannot do what they
would unless assisted by the worldly goods of
those who are unable to give their time, to
give themselves to this the greatest act of
love that can be performed, the greatest need
this world has, the assistance of the dying.
By doing this we do an undying work, a sure
work, for if we obtain for a sinner a happy
death, there can be no relapse, the work is
done for eternity.

But we can help to beautify a good death
as well as save a soul from a bad one.   We
often visit a sick person, and finding them in
good dispositions, we do not think it necessary
to say anything to them.   Why not try to
teach them the " True Devotion"?   Why not
try to explain it to them in a few words, such
as these : " Would you not like to be Mary's
own, given to our Lady as entirely as Jesus
was, at least as much as you can, for we know
we never can belong to her so entirely as Jesus
was?   He chose her from His home in heaven,
He came and gave Himself wholly, entirely
to her, He was her Child, He put Himself in

her hands. Will you do the same? Would you not like to spend the remaining days of your sickness in close imitation of Jesus? Then put yourself entirely in Mary's hands, depend upon her as Jesus did, and nearer and closer to Jesus and to her through the endless ages of eternity will you be for having been closer in union with Jesus during the last days of your life on earth. You will grow in grace in a few days by this devotion more than in many years without it, so we are told by holy, saintly souls who have practised it." Thus in few words could we explain the devotion our Lady loves. In few words, likewise, we could explain how the "Act of Consecration" is made. Remind them of the mystery of the Annunciation, tell them after receiving Holy Communion to give themselves to our Lady in union with Jesus, and to ask Him to show them how to give themselves to our Lady as He did, to consecrate themselves to her maternal care as He did. It is done by an act of the will, though a set form of words may be used, saying that henceforth they have nothing of their own, that even their spiritual goods they give to Mary, for she is Mistress of all they have, as well as Mother of their heart and soul.

Do not then let us forget that we are doing

a great work when we add to the *beauty* of a
death-bed, as well as when we prevent the
death-bed being a place of sacrilege, of utter
detestation and abhorrence, a place where God
has cursed His creature.   Besides preventing
this terrible calamity, let us strive to render
the death-bed of those we attend a place most
beautiful in the sight of heaven and earth.
Let it be as an altar prepared for sacrifice;
let the living victim lie there ready to immo-
late itself to God; let us strive to inspire into
those we are able to influence the holiest
thoughts of death; let us, by kind words of
advice and prayer, prevent their marring the
beauty of that grand scene by impatience,
self-love, want of resignation, or the shadow of
distrust of God's goodness and mercy.   They
can be told of it kindly if we see anything of
this, and they will be glad to be told rather
than disappoint or offend God in the slightest
at such a time.   Their minds may be rather
weakened by sickness, and they may need
reminding; simply humouring their infirmities would only do them harm.   Be patient
with their weaknesses, but still do not always
hide them from them; raise their thoughts to
higher, better things if they are inclined to
tend to earth and worldly affairs. Do, in fact,
all that lies in your power to render that

moment what it should be to God, most pleasing, most precious in His sight; do all that you can to make that death-bed a place where God blessed His child with unutterable love, and proclaimed it His own, His very own, and in folding it to Himself, imprinted upon it the kiss of everlasting peace. God grant this to us when we come to die, and God grant our Mother may be there to help us at that momentous moment upon which our eternity depends.

### PRAYER FOR THE EIGHTY THOUSAND WHO DAILY DIE.

Jesus, by the love Thou bearest the Heart of Thy Mother, have pity on the dying. Jesus, by Thine infinite compassion, compassionate and spare the dying. Jesus, by the love borne by the Eternal Father for the souls He has created, save sinners dying.

---

## TWENTY-SEVENTH DAY.

### The Love of our Lady for the Sorrowful.

Poor mourners of earth, mourn on, murmur not, for there is a Mother above looking upon you with exceeding love, a Mother who knows well what sorrow is, for she herself has suffered as none other ever did, save One, and He her own Divine Son. If there is a time when our Mother loves us more than at another, it is when we are suffering; if there is ever a time when she restrains her desire to show herself as a tender Mother, and to impart to us the happy assurance that we are pleasing in the sight of the Most High, it is then, when our hearts are wrung with grief, our souls writhing, one may say, in bitter agony, at those times of terrible trial which most of us have some experience of in our own lifetime; but she restrains for a time the natural longing of her Maternal Heart to comfort and console; she holds back, as it were, that almost sensible perception of her presence which is such a joy to her children; at least, I would say, she acts thus with those souls who are strong enough to bear it, and to whom she knows it will be of benefit; from such she withholds the comfort she sends others; she often leaves her more favoured child alone in its desolation for days, weeks, perhaps months, according as, watchful, loving Mother that she is, she sees it is able to bear the rack on which love has placed it. But our Mother finds few of her children able to remain long without some sensible consolation, therefore in her goodness

and tender compassion she solaces them, she
consoles them, and for the most part, as we
may believe, and as our dear Lord Himself
was consoled, by the ministry of angels. Precious suffering, precious sorrow, would that
we understood its value better, would that we
understood better how to suffer. We must all
suffer, I repeat it: would that we suffered
well; it would indeed bring us blessings in
this world, but far greater in the next; it
would be better for ourselves, and better too
for others.

If we would know why Mary so loves to
see her children suffering patiently, we must
look on Jesus suffering, we must see Jesus in
agony of body and soul, we must see Jesus
shedding blood for us. As we do this in daily
meditation there springs up in our hearts a
longing to be like Him, to be in real union
with Him, not union of mere sentiment and
feeling alone, but real union of act. Yes; if
we meditate well this desire arises in our
hearts, this first commencement of sanctity,
when piety ceases to be merely an affection,
and is really put into effect. Now this desire,
even when at its highest in the hearts of
saints, is but a faint shadow of the feeling and
desire in our Lady's Heart that her children
should imitate Jesus, should be like Him,

should be united to Him with a real veritable union, a grand union which in the saints rises to a melting of their whole being into Jesus, for Jesus lives in them so completely that their natural selves seem dead, Jesus lives and reigns within them. Now Jesus desires to live in all hearts; Mary is anxious to prepare her children for this, and she knows that it is by well-borne suffering alone that corrupt nature can be crucified, and the Spirit of Jesus live triumphant on the ruins of self.

Jesus suffering! We have all sorrowed, thinking of our Love in sorrow. What a pain it is to see one we love in sorrow. We have all felt this pain, but we have felt very little of it indeed in comparison with what Mary felt. She looked upon Jesus, and as she saw His loving, gentle, sensitive nature so terribly outraged, so sadly grieved, her love was poured out upon Jesus the more. His love for the human race showed itself by the suffering He endured for them, and our grateful love of Him must also be shown by our suffering with Him and for Him, and the more we suffer bravely, patiently, generously, hiddenly, the more will our Mother love us for His sake. Her tender Heart will yearn towards us with untold love, untold at least on earth. Yes; we must wait for heaven for Mary to tell us

how she loves us, how she loves those who
have suffered for the love of God, who have
mourned and sorrowed gently, quietly, as she
herself did. Then shall we find that having
mourned on earth, in heaven we are indeed
blessed and comforted in a manner that here
we know not of, "for eye had not seen, nor
ear heard, neither had it entered into the
heart of man" to form any conception of it.

"Mother of sorrows! sweet patient Mother!
comfort the comfortless ones, by teaching them
the grand lesson, the greatest lesson to be
learned in these troublous times,—how to
suffer.

"How best can we learn this lesson? Reveal thy sorrowing Heart to us. Those can
speak who have leaned their suffering souls
upon Mary's pierced Heart, and drawn comfort
and consolation and strength from it. Mary!
thy Heart is beautiful! beautiful from its
purity, but beautiful likewise from the suffering, patient suffering, which it endured. We
do love thy sweet compassionate Heart, dear
Mother! If thou wert simply the glorious
Queen of Heaven,—we might say more even,
—if thou wert Mother of God, without being
our sweet suffering Mother Mary, could we
love thee the same? But if any heart was
ever crushed, if any heart was ever bitterly

wrung, it has been the Heart of our own dear
Mother.    That is the thought we think as we
press our weary hearts on her breast, and draw
comfort and consolation from the most suffering
creature, the most suffering, the most sweet of
all human beings.

" We think what we cannot speak of thy
sufferings, sweet Mother! of thy fair sensitive
nature, so wrung, so tortured ; of thy sweet
womanly, Motherly Heart, so terribly tried,
so delicate, so tender, and so fearfully wrung.
Oh Mary ! our sorrows come upon us unfore-
seen ; if we knew the calamities that would
befall us our lives would be a misery of
anticipation.    And yet the long, long years of
thy life, with the sword, the one self-same
sword piercing thy soul, the very sight of
Jesus causing thee more and more, as love
grew in thee, deeper and deeper pain.    We,
with our poor weak love, we could not bear
to touch our dear Lord's hand, for the joy of
that contact would thrill us with anguish as
we thought of the nail that would one day
pierce it.    We could not, if we had lived in
the time of Jesus's Human Life, have looked
in His sweet face, have met His loving gaze,
blended with a vision of the Man of Sorrows,
with the wan, white, grief-stricken face, the
sorrowful eyes.    Could we have borne this ?

We think not. But Mary bore this; day after day, week after week, year after year, she lived on her life of love and suffering.

" Oh, let us imitate her; let us love the Mother who lived so lovely a life, and let us strive to imitate her. We all in our measure have the opportunity, the means of doing so. Do let us entreat this grace of graces. Plead, sweet Mother of sorrows, before the throne of God, for the sorrowing. Take pity, dear Mother of pity and compassion, upon us poor mourners of earth, and after having suffered here, lead thy children with joy to Jesus's throne, to receive the reward of suffering on earth, the joy of Jesus. Yes, in heaven Jesus rejoices in the fruit of His suffering, and we too shall rejoice in ours. If we are brave on earth we shall go to heaven, not alone, but countless souls with us, and rejoice with those we love on the bosom of God for evermore. No more shall we see those we love suffering, but rejoice in their joy as our own."—" *Our Lady's Comfort to the Sorrowful,*" *Preface, pp.* **xviii.-xxi.**

## TWENTY-EIGHTH DAY.

### The Love of our Lady for Humility.

Our Lady's love of humility! Yes, truly,
in all, above all her other virtues—queen as
it were of all the rest—do we see the sweet
humility of Mary, so unearthly, so unlike
anything of this world, so like the humility
of Jesus; that propensity, that earnest longing to be hidden from the sight of creatures,
and to live only in the sight of the Creator.
Oh, that strong desire of Mary to be hidden
and unknown, so unlike all human desire, so
supernatural, so entirely contrary to the
spirit of the world. Why is it, since we know
and firmly believe how dear this virtue is in
the sight of God, why is it that we do not
strive more earnestly to possess it?

How little true humility is there in the
world; how little love of the hidden life;
how little secresy of intercourse between the
soul of the creature and its Creator. Oh, let
Mary's own learn this lesson from their
Mother. Let them imbibe this love of humility from the sweet Heart of Mary, for if
they would live in union with their Mother,

they must love to be hidden, they must love
to be unknown. Besides the humility of the
soul, which loves to lose itself in the bosom
of the Creator, because of His unspeakable
goodness and greatness, and to be unknown to
creatures that it may be known only to God,
there is another form of humility to be considered, springing from the thought of the
nothingness and sinfulness of the creature,
which is but another name for self-knowledge,
the truthful knowledge of ourselves. Mary
ever saw herself in the light of God's truth;
she lived ever with a clear conception of what
she was of herself; she saw her own nothingness; she saw nothing in herself worthy of a
thought except God's grace in her, and the
wondrous blessings He had lavished on her,
and thanked Him for it,—in one word, she saw
herself only as a creature of God. She could
not indeed see herself apart from Him, for
she never had been apart from Him during
one single instant of her existence, as we unfortunately have been; and this fact, that we
have been, at least for one short period of our
lives, if not for more, not God's children, at en-
mity with Him, we should consider to our own
humiliation; we do not consider it sufficiently,
and grow humble under the thought. The
Saints who had never stained their baptismal

carcely utter
om the know
efittingly, cou
nce; if *our* l
he pure, bea
ave felt? A
o fathom it.
eavours, our
uto that pure
Jary, will no
rish to discon
till strive to
ver rememb
evertheless G
   We will an

... —
— l....l
—— ....
. .... .j
.... ....
....ing .
— .... p
.... ...
.... ...
. .... .
. .... n
.. lawf..
.. e, only
.. ka.
: humili.
that if w
will find
.. Moth
and thee,
we do .
. be most
.. love ..
virtue, fo
. May .
virtue, an
....ceit, ..
.he love .
God's vio

innocence, wept and mourned at the thought
of their having been born with the stain of
original sin upon them.    We think such
piety overstrained and exaggerated.   Would
that we had their knowledge of God's purity
and of our own fallen state, and the misery of
being separated from God, even for an instant, so that we too might learn humility
from the consideration; that we too might
become humble, as the Saints are, from the
daily meditation of what we are and what
God is.

We must say again what we have said so
often in other works, " humility is truth,"
and the reason God loves humility is because
of His great love of truth.   We shall grow in
this great grace of humility if we keep close
to Mary, our lowly humble Mother.    We
feel lowly when we but think of her,—we feel
that we love to be hidden when we sit at the
feet of Mary; we learn from her a lesson we
do not perhaps so easily learn elsewhere, a
lesson of what we are, of what God is.    We
learn by meditating on Jesus in Mary, how
Jesus loved to hide Himself, how God hid
Himself; we learn to seek to hide ourselves
too, and to live only for love, for love of God.
It is the truly humble soul that loves God
most.    There is a secrecy, a hiddenness, a

certain modesty as regards itself (if we may use the expression), a certain fear of being seen, in the chaste humble soul, which shows that it is very close to God.

Thus was our dear Mother in her sweet humility, shrinking within herself, away from the eyes of all, hiding the beauty which she nevertheless knew she possessed, keeping it for God alone. Oh, God! may we imitate her, may we thus live, and may our lives ever send forth sweet incense, sweet music,—but for Thee, O God, and not for creatures, for Thyself, and when lawfully and rightly for others, still for Thee, only that we may please others for Thy sake. Sweet Mother, we know that without humility we cannot please God. We know that if we are truly humble, our least actions will find favour in His sight. Make us then, dear Mother, humble, hidden children of God and thee, loving to hide ourselves and what we do from those around, that we may thus be most cherished children of Jesus; may He love us more as He sees us grow in this virtue, for the sake of which He so loved thee. May we be Mary-like in this thy special virtue, and as the world rolls on in its deadly conceit, and pride, and pomp, and vanity, and the love of display, may we, imitating thee—God's violet—grow in lowliness, in hiddenness, in sweetness to God, because we modestly hide, as far as we may, from the gaze and knowledge of the world the graces and gifts He bestows on us.

We will sit daily at thy feet, sweet Mother, and learn our lesson of humility from thee. We will perform acts of humility to obtain this grand virtue. We will submit to any humiliating process our dear heavenly Mother may impose upon us: we will be patient under failures; we will be forgiving and gentle with those who injure us; we will submit to be humbled in the eyes of creatures, that we may grow great in the sight of our Creator. We will allow ourselves to be crushed, if need be, for it is thus we can grow in humility; we will cling closer to our Mother when, in her love for our immortal souls, she keeps us low, when she permits us to be hard tried, humbled, tempted, almost to despair; I say tempted, for we cannot really despair while we cling to her. All these trials will be for our good, we shall know it hereafter; we shall know it even now. For we shall find that we love our sweet Mother more for her seeming severity; we shall see how she helped us through what appeared almost insuperable temptations, and when we have come forth from the crucifying process, we shall throw ourselves with glad hearts on our Mother's bosom, and cry out in our joy and thanksgiving : " It is good for me that thou hast humbled me, for before I was humbled I offended." Mother of Mercy, thou art most merciful in the crosses thou dost send us and help us to bear; we could not bear them without thee, Mary our Mother, but thou makest all things sweet when thou art with us; thou makest this life even so sweet that at the thought of leaving it we lingeringly look back when we think that in the next life we cannot suffer, and feeling almost regret at the thought instead of joy, as indeed we ought. But Thou knowest what is best, dear Lord, and when Thou willest it, when Thou hast tested us and tried us, and humbled us sufficiently, call us, and we will come to Thee. Come for us, and we will go to Thee, to be with Thee in the land where live only those who are meek and humble of heart.

## TWENTY-NINTH DAY.

### The Love of our Lady for the Truthful.

It may be thought that, drawing now to the end of our Lady's month, if we begin to speak of her love for the various virtues, we shall need another month in which to read the conferences that would be needed; but such is not our purpose. We have picked out this virtue of truthfulness because, (we hardly like to say it,) it seems with some to be scarcely regarded as a virtue, and because this virtue of simplicity, of straightforwardness, of truthfulness, should be an especial mark of Mary's own, and pervade their entire spirit. They must combat against the glaring deceit of the world, they must draw from the Heart of their Mother her love for the truth, they must be simple as doves if they would be in accord with her Heart, if they would be dear, as they surely wish to be, to that pure, truthful, holy Heart of Mary. We must look to heaven, where dwells the God of Truth; we must draw near to Mary, Mother of Truth Incarnate; we must live in the company of the angels of truth, winging their way through

this world of sin and deceit; we must live as
they do, not tainted by its sinfulness, not
deceived by its sounding hollowness, not
cheated by its false lights and glittering show.
Could we imagine those bright spirits de-
ceiving us, or striving to deceive one another?
And yet how sad the sight we witness daily
amongst ourselves. I am not speaking of
sinners. No; we cannot wonder that they
fear not to speak falsely; but of those who
are really good in so many ways, but yet
have so little scruple about the truth in their
ordinary conversation, who seem even to think
their utter want of Christian simplicity a
clever accomplishment, and who, if even they
say what they really mean, without reserve
and without dissimulation, do so as it were by
accident. They may think, as they evidently
do, that there is no harm in this; but a day
will come when they will bitterly rue it.
Would that they could see their mistake.
They may be mortified, they may have good
qualities, they may be in a way aiming at
perfection, but they never will reach it; they
are not even on the road of the saints so long
as they use their lips to frame words of dissimulation, and are so utterly devoid of the
simplicity of the saints. We cannot do better
than quote here from that great lover of Mary,

and her faithful servant, he who was so truly one of Mary's own, Father Faber:

" Scripture reveals to us quite in startling language the intensity of God's hatred of a lie. But there are hundreds of things which do not amount to lies, yet which are contrary to the beautiful perfection of simplicity.  There is a speech and a silence, there are looks, manners, permissions, concealments, dubious smiles, pretended inadvertences, unworthy conventions, and intentional distractions, which grieve the Holy Spirit, and make sad ravages of an interior soul, though they are far short of absolute falsehood.  I think it is St. Augustine who says somewhere, that the devil so envied God the possession of His beloved Word, that he strove to mimic the Eternal Generation of the Son, and to produce a word himself, which should be, as far as was in his power, consubstantial with himself, and that he straightway begot a lie; so that a lie is the devil's word, a daring, foul, and loathsome imitation of the Ever-glorious and Only-begotten Son of God.  This explains the intensity of God's hatred of a lie.  This is an exposition of our Lord's name for the devil, the father of lies.

" Now all this may be recommended to the notice even of spiritual persons.   They offend

God and do themselves a mischief by untruth,
not in the shape of falsehood, but in the shape
of want of simplicity. If you would be perfect, you must be truthful to a scruple. A
hair's-breadth of deceit must be to you as if it
were a mile of positive untruth.

"Persons professing to aim at a life of
union with God, and whose discretion fails of
being supernatural because it falls short of
simplicity, are sometimes heard to quote what
writers of moral theology teach about the
permissions of equivocations, amphibology,
and mental reserve. I wish it could be rudely
forced home upon them how shocking this is!
Moral theology is not a system of ascetics, or
a code of the counsels of perfection. The writers are engaged in showing either what is the
very least of good dispositions on which we
may rest a reluctant absolution, so as to attract
sinners more powerfully to God, and to advance the kingdom of Christ to the furthest
confines of sheer possibility, and to carry the
Precious Blood to the uttermost limit to which
it will go; or else they are occupied in ex-
plaining for the guidance of the priest how far
an action may be imperfect, and what amount
of unworthiness it may contain, without being
an absolute breach of any of God's laws, and so
subjecting the offender to certain spiritual

punishments and disabilities. Men might as
well model their kindliness to the poor, sick,
and sorrowing around them, on the manual of
a justice of the peace as practise spirituality
on a treatise of moral theology. Forgive my
repeating it. Get out of these little untruth-
fulnesses. When a man says in defence of
himself, It is not a sin, he is making a public
profession of abandoning the pursuit of perfection. Remember the maxim of a holy man,
' Le grand obstacle du progrès spirituel est de
ne s'abstenir que de ce qui paroît offense de
Dieu, et de faire sans scrupule ce qui se peut
faire sans crime.' But of one thing I am quite
clear, that many persons aiming at perfection,
practising mental prayer and performing
bodily mortifications, come to a dead standstill
because of their want of scruple about insin-
cerities far short of untruth. Diplomacy of
manner, way, and speech, circuitous routes for
courtesy's sake, giving things the wrong
names, and being silent when silence is really
speech, these things are undoing men's sanctity, and causing saints to break in the mould,
and frustrating beautiful purposes of grace
every day. And so subtle is the delusion that
when men feel that something is wrong in
them, but cannot depict it, they wake up as
it were to some rude savage theories of mis-

placed and inopportune fraternal correction, or think to compensate for their cowardly double-dealing and double-tonguedness by the misplaced effusions of a vulgar candour. The devil will turn their attention in any direction rather than the right one. He dearly loves those little plausibilities and diplomacies. They are caverns where he finds congenial darkness even when the rays of grace are beaming brightest on the soul, and where he lies hid till the splendours have faded into the usual grey twilight of a soul that is but half for God."*

There is, however, another kind of untruthfulness which we have carefully to avoid, for it is most displeasing to our dear Mother. It could hardly exist, in fact it could not be in one of Mary's own, who is really living in her spirit, really walking in her footsteps. We mention it for the sake of those who are commencing their journey, who have taken but a few steps in the Path of Mary, as a warning that they may not stray into this sad sidepath, this dangerous deceitful road of self-deception, of false devotion, of imagining they are seeking God when they are principally seeking themselves with a certain kind of

* Father Faber, "Blessed Sacrament," p. 242.

spirituality made up according to their own form and fashion.

Spirituality is not something imaginary and unreal; on the contrary, it is the most real of all realities, it is *realizing* the truth in our minds and hearts and outward conduct.  It is no doubt a fact that some people, wishing to be spiritual, do put themselves into imaginary states, and strive to attain perfection in their own way, but they are not really spiritual, they are very much mistaken people, they are following a Will-o'-the-wisp.  Why do we strive to imagine this or that, or to be this and that, instead of striving to realize what is truthful, to be very simple, that is, very truthful ?   We hear of people who will perhaps for some months be practising one kind of spirituality in consequence of something they have read, and are very pleased with.  They, without consideration, embrace it, imagining they have found a great treasure, are very earnest for a time, and then gradually lose their fervour, and next year you will find them in quite another state, and the following year they have changed again, and are following some fresh mystic writer who has tickled their fancy.  Converts are liable to this delusion, or rather series of delusions, for God certainly cannot follow them in their various

fancies, their devotion cannot come from His
Holy Spirit. They have gone on from one
thing to another, according to their own
imaginations; God did not lead them, I might
say they have not given Him an opportunity
of doing so. Now I would not wish to make
any one uneasy or scrupulous. Many good-
hearted people have fallen into this mistake.
I do not say they have sinned, or that their
whole spiritual life was a delusion. Oh, no;
they were doubtless in a state of grace, but
their mistake has been, being too desirous of
pleasing themselves in their devotions, thinking too little what God's will for them was,
and by the imaginary states of prayer they
have put themselves into keeping God's Holy
Spirit away from them rather than drawing
Him towards them, which should be their
great object. We cannot possibly think that
God will be in these various spiritual states
they put themselves into. Beginners in the
spiritual life, and converts, should both of
them have one principal thought in their
minds, strive for three special graces, and
they are these,—contrition, humility, and
an earnest seeking the will of God in all
things. They should put themselves before
God as the novice-mistress of Blessed Margaret Mary counselled her to do: "Put
9

yourself before God as a blank sheet of paper on which He may write." Wonderful advice! Would we all had the Blessed Margaret's humility to follow it; we should be different to what we are. But we *will* put ourselves forward, not alone before our fellow-creatures, but even before the adorable Majesty of God. We will not sink down in a truthful state of nothingness before Him, and listen to the truths He will tell us, or rather implant within us, since He uses no word. It would almost seem as if we thought that we can tell Him a great deal more than He can us. We come into His presence with our own way of thinking, with our own ideas, with a set spirituality of our own, and we are therefore not at all in a fit state for His Holy Spirit to work upon, and God therefore cannot give us the light He would wish to give. We must therefore pray for that docile spirit out of which God forms His saints. We must be truthful to ourselves, to God, to creatures; and by truthful I simply mean humble, with some little sense of what we are, and who God is, and an earnest desire of being taught by Him. We will place ourselves before God in our simple, natural nakedness of soul, divested as we are of all supernatural good, unless clothed with His grace; but when softened, melted, liquefied, as it were, capable of being formed, because God's Holy Spirit has banished what was rigid, stiff, and hard in us, then will our Mother mould us at her will, praised be God, and then we shall come from her fair hands new creatures, renewed in spirit, in mind, filled with God's Spirit of truth, incapable of deceit; and because we are truthful, dearly will our God love us, richly will He reward us in heaven for our watchfulness over ourselves here, our conscientious endeavour to be children of the God of Truth. Trouble it will certainly cost us to combat with our nature, which is inclined to deceit, especially if we have contracted a habit of insincerity and dissimulation. But we must pray, we must watch, we must weigh our words before we utter them, we must penance ourselves in some way whenever we transgress.

It is well for us to suffer, however little, for our love of truth; the martyrs suffered the rack and the halter for it. God will bless us, even in this life, with the blessing He gives His most cherished ones, that blessing by which they find the God of Truth everywhere, in every time and place, for truth has shown them that God alone is, that He is before all, above all, in all,—truth has shown them their God, ever present with them.

Such was the reward of Mary's faith, which is the light of truth, never to lose sight of God. She lived, sweet Mother, a simple life of truth, or her life would not have been beautiful as it was. Is it possible to imagine that holy Virgin speaking to some neighbour with words of dissimulation, words which, if not altogether false, are intended to conceal what is really passing in the speaker's mind, words sometimes of positive deceit, such as are at times spoken even by those who are professing to serve God with their whole hearts.

It is indeed painful to witness such things, painful to hear those who are adepts at it, and do it without shame; painful to hear those who are not so practised, but who nevertheless do it, though with some shame and confusion. Too well do we know that expression in the face of those who are attempting to deceive; is it Mary-like? is it candid and open? Shall it ever be seen in one of Mary's own? Watch our Lady's words, how simple they are, how straightforward, how to the purpose: "How can this be done?" she said to the Angel, with simple straightforwardness, no beating about the bush, no roundabout expressions, but when she did speak she did it simply, and what she really thought and felt she said; when her heart rejoiced she said so in her grand outburst: "My soul doth magnify the Lord;" when wearied, tried, in uncertainty about God's ways, in extreme of suffering, if she speaks at all, her lips must utter what is in her Heart, "Why hast Thou done so to us?" Yes, in sweet simplicity Mary questioned God; she spoke her mind, and she shows her suffering: "Thy father and I have sought Thee sorrowing."

Ah, Mother, what can thy children do but sit and listen at thy feet, to learn thy ways, to imbibe thy spirit, to learn thy loves, and learn to love them too, and thus to love thy love of truth, and resolve that their lives shall not shame their Mother, but glorify her ways, so that they may be marked out in this world, and known as Mary's own, since they are upright, simple, truthful, and therefore pleasing in the sight of God and man.

## THIRTIETH DAY.

### The Love of the Heart of our Lady for her Son.

[As we are now at the close of Mary's month, let us once more turn our thoughts to the greatest of her loves, her love for her divine Son, the glorious subject we never can have enough of. We can never grow weary in contemplating the love of the Mother for her Son.]

"My Mother!" "My Son! my Child!" "My Mother!" spoke Jesus. "My Son! my Child!" spoke the Mother of Jesus, the Mother of God. "Holy Mary, Mother of God," we cry to thee, sweet Mother, day by day, hour by hour,—we thus address thee, and yet do we sit silently pondering still what the words "Mother of God" must mean. We love God, we ever meditate on our God, the God Who made us, and our hearts so burn with love that we feel at times afraid of this our love; we fear lest we should go to excess, lest it should lead us to say or do before others something which would betray us, something strange or exaggerated, for we love to hide our love as Mary did; but we do love our God more than we could say. What

would it be then if we held our God in our
arms, if we pressed Him to our breast? Oh,
Mary, what didst thou feel when thou be-
camest the Mother of God? It is wrapt in
mystery; there is a veil thrown over it. It
is more of Heaven than earth, and not to be
exposed to the rude gaze of the world. Mary
speaks once of her inward joy, her rapture;
she tells us that her soul magnified her Lord,
that her spirit rejoiced in God her Saviour.
She tells us much in her beautiful canticle of
praise and thanksgiving, much, that is, to those
who meditate on it—for her words are very
brief—and then she is silent. We hear no
more of her joy; her next word is of her sorrow: "Thy father and I have sought Thee
sorrowing." She held the Desired of all nations in her arms, and we hear no word from
her lips; she presses Him to her with her
fond maternal love, but she tells us not of what
she felt as she gazed upon her God, Whom
she held in her arms a helpless Infant; "the
Virgin Mother and the Child Divine," the
one object, in all Christian ages, of the intense
delight of all who love God, the unwearied
subject of meditation of all contemplatives.
Mary, Mother; Jesus, Son;—Mother, open
thy Heart and reveal to us some little of thy
love for Jesus as thy Son, thy own, Him Who

was All in all to thee, Him whose beauteous Body was formed from thy Heart's blood by the Holy Spirit, the precious Pearl of the ever Blessed Trinity, whom thou broughtest forth into this world, the Only-Begotten of the Eternal Father, and yet thy Son, sweet Mother, thy Son, fed from thy breasts, nourished by thee, nursed and tended by thee, dependent on thee.   Mothers alone know that peculiar love they have for those they bring into this world, to whom they give life, their children.   Then, O Mother of mothers, what was thy love for thy Child, Who was all thy Child, Who had no earthly father, that wondrous Child, who was God as well as man? We love our Jesus, Mother, we do indeed love Him ; but love Him as we will, and think of thy love as we will, we seem to come no nearer to understanding thy love of Him ; it seems farther and farther away from our cold hearts the more we try to draw nearer to it. We receive Jesus in Holy Communion ; we hold Him close to our hearts.   We kneel, awed, stilled, silent, and Jesus does His work within us ; we are quiet, we are in communion, real intimate communion with our God. Do we feel in even the slightest degree some feelings of love akin to those our Mother felt with Jesus within her, or with Jesus pressed to her breast? Yes, and yet no. Yes, there is some sort of love similar to Mary's, and yet no, for that very little we have of love shows us how far beyond is the love of the Mother above all mothers,—the love of Mary for Jesus: it is like a sudden ray of light, a sudden flash on the mountain top, which, for a moment lets us see a vast expanse before us, all lit up, but far away.

Ah, Mother, it seems foolish to have attempted to write of thy love for Jesus; easier can we understand thy love for God, thy Creator, than thy love for God, thy Son; for the love of a creature for its Creator is a natural love, though by grace made supernatural too, reason alone can, to some degree, bring it home to our minds and hearts; but the other love is supernatural, all above nature, for reason without faith knows nothing of it.

We leave it, then, dear Mother, with this determination, that day after day we will meditate upon thee and thy love for Jesus thy Son, until we learn some little more of thy love; we will strive, meanwhile, to be as close to thee, to give ourselves as entirely to thee as we can, to be as much like Jesus to thee as we can, and try and love thee as much like Jesus as we can, that thus we may please thee and endear ourselves to thy sweet Maternal Heart.

Mother of Jesus, I come to claim thee as my own Mother, by consecrating myself entirely to thee. In union, in imitation of Jesus, I desire to give myself to thee, to love thee, to depend upon thee with Jesus, who was more thine than I shall ever be, though I give myself as wholly to thee as I can, that I may be made like to Him. May I ever love thee with a child-like love; may I love thee with a Jesu's-love. Show thyself a Mother to me; show that thou acceptest the offering of myself that I now make to thee. I am not worthy to be thy child, I have nought to offer thee worthy of thy acceptance. My heart I consecrate to thy Maternal Heart: but my heart is sinful, stained; it is filled with roots of sin. I then join my heart to the Heart of Jesus. I offer to thee the Sacred Heart that so loves thee, that is indeed also so beloved by thee, so more thy Heart than thy own. I can give thee no greater joy than in the offering of that Heart, as Jesus has had no greater joy from this earth than in the offering of thy pure Heart to Him. Thus in offering my poor unworthy heart to Jesus, do thou, dear Mother, lend thine to me, that united with it, it may be

less unworthy of His acceptance; and in
offering my heart to thee, sweet Mother, I
beg of Jesus to give me His; and thus in
union with the Son of God, made Son of
Mary, I give to thee, for time and eternity,
my heart and soul, my whole being, that
henceforth, both on earth, and I trust in
heaven, I may be ever known, in union with
Jesus, as "child of Mary." May the Holy
Spirit form me to true likeness of Jesus.
May the Eternal Father claim me as true
child of the Son of His Love.

---

## THIRTY-FIRST DAY.

### The Love of our Lady for Prayer.

We will finish our thoughts upon the
various loves of the Heart of Mary with a
consideration of her love of prayer. It is not
that we have finished thinking of the various
loves that filled the Heart of God's child of
love, Mary. Very little indeed has been said
of that which we feel should be said. There
come before our minds so very many loves in
Mary's Heart that we have not even touched

upon, as for example, her love of virginity, her love of the sacraments, and so we should wander on and on from one to another, not knowing which to dwell upon as most useful for her children to think and meditate about, though doubtless all would be useful, and each would yield some special fruit. Certainly her love of the sacraments would be a most useful subject for reflection. Would that we could view these wonderful operations of grace as Mary did; would that we understood them with some little of her intelligence; would that we could see their work in souls as she does, the marvellous manner in which they purify and beautify them; and then indeed we should esteem them and run to them; then indeed the Church would present to God followers of Christ in deed, and not in name only, as too many, far too many Christians are; then indeed would detraction, backbiting, untruthfulness, selfishness, and the many evils Catholics give way to with so little scruple, cease in a great measure their baneful effects. Yes; if the sacraments were reverenced and frequented as they should be, soon would Christendom raise itself from the many plagues which at present harass and distress it; its bleeding wounds would be healed. But the consideration of this subject would need a separate book; it would not do to skim it over lightly as we have been obliged to do with the subjects we have meditated on in the present volume.

Now, as briefly as we can, we will consider our Lady's love of prayer, her own continual prayer to God, and her love that we too should pray, her earnest desire that her children should imitate her and be like herself, ardent lovers of prayer. If the thought of our Lady's prayer, and of God's love of her prayer, should induce any one to commence at once to imitate her in this respect, we shall think we have, by God's grace, accomplished an undying work, for the effect of true heartfelt prayer is eternal. The soul that prays well will save itself, and God alone knows how many souls besides itself.

To view our Lady praying on earth as God viewed her from heaven, let us turn to Him, and ask a special grace, a light from His Holy Spirit. We will try to keep closer to our God, that we may view this world as He views it, that we may contemplate Mary as she walked this earth, holy, upright, simple, pure, beautiful, God's spotless creature. There she was in her simple cottage, intent upon her needlework, her household duties, but in the midst of all never forgetful of her one

great duty as a creature of God, to praise
Him as such, to thank Him for having created
her, to thank Him for His eternal love of
her, and then, forgetting herself, thanking
Him with that Heart of love of hers for His
own great glory, for His great goodness, His
beauty, His infinite perfections, His power,
His majesty, His might. All this, and immensely more than we can conceive, would
come before Mary, were ever before her, and
her heart and soul ever rejoiced in the living
God, and yet so simply, ever as she went
about her work, speaking kind words to her
neighbours, doing little acts of charity, attentive to the minutest duties in the house, for
nothing was forgotten. Oh, beautiful life of
Mary; lovingly we look upon it, and wonder;
and wistfully we linger over it, and whisper to
our guardian angels that we long to copy it,
and ask them to show us and to teach us how
we may. The only one way we can do so is
by uniting continued prayer with all we do
and in whatever place we may be. Oh, the
beautiful incense of that continual prayer of
Mary. Would that one little flame of love
like hers might shoot upward from our hearts
to the throne of God, were it but once in our
lives. Would that our hearts were, before
God, filled to overflowing with love a little

like Mary's, love for her God Himself, and
love for God's creatures. And in truth we
could if we would make our hearts resemble
Mary's somewhat more than they now do.
Why do we not? It is from slothfulness,
from carelessness, from want of guard of our
senses, that we are so unrecollected, and
therefore so soon lose the graces we receive,
and cannot keep within us the spirit of prayer.
A gift of prayer is one of God's greatest gifts ;
a true spirit of prayer indeed seems one of
His rarest gifts, and yet He would gladly give
it to all. How is it so few possess it? how is
it that there is so little of the spirit of prayer
to be found? As we have just said, it is from
carelessness, from real supineness. Now what
is valuable has to be acquired, and what is of
the greatest value cannot as a rule be acquired
without much effort. God respects the laws
He Himself has established. He has not
made them to be set aside, which they would
be were He to work in us by supernatural
means without our own co-operation, without
our using the natural means, the faculties, the
memory, the understanding, the will which
He has given us to be used in His service.

Now the difficulty of acquiring a habit of
recollection, which is indispensable for a spirit

great duty as a creature of God, to praise Him as such, to thank Him for having created her, to thank Him for His eternal love of her, and then, forgetting herself, thanking Him with that Heart of love of hers for His own great glory, for His great goodness, His beauty, His infinite perfections, His power, His majesty, His might. All this, and immensely more than we can conceive, would come before Mary, were ever before her, and her heart and soul ever rejoiced in the living God, and yet so simply, ever as she went about her work, speaking kind words to her neighbours, doing little acts of charity, attentive to the minutest duties in the house, for nothing was forgotten. Oh, beautiful life of Mary; lovingly we look upon it, and wonder; and wistfully we linger over it, and whisper to our guardian angels that we long to copy it, and ask them to show us and to teach us how we may. The only one way we can do so is by uniting continued prayer with all we do and in whatever place we may be. Oh, the ... se of that continual prayer of ... that one little flame of love ... upward from our ... God, were it but ... that our he... to overflowing

like Mary's, love for her God Himself, an
love for God's creatures. And in truth w
could if we would make our hearts resembl
Mary's somewhat more than they now d
Why do we not? It is from slothfulnes
from carelessness, from want of guard of ou
senses, that we are so unrecollected, an
therefore so soon lose the graces we receive
and cannot keep within us the spirit of prayer
A gift of prayer is one of God's greatest gifts
a true spirit of prayer indeed seems one o
His rarest gifts, and yet He would gladly give
it to all. How is it so few possess it? how i
it that there is so little of the spirit of praye
to be found? As we have just said, it is from
carelessness, from real supineness. Now wha
is valuable has to be acquired, and what is o
the greatest value cannot as a rule be acquire
without much effort. God respects the law
He Himself has established. He has
made them to be

of prayer, is a fact acknowledged by most
who have succeeded in acquiring it, but this
difficulty can be surmounted by perseverance,
by using well all our natural means. It may
perhaps take time, but in the end the difficulty
will certainly be overcome. It was by the
persevering exercise of the natural powers of
his mind and heart, in co-operation with
divine grace, which perhaps was given in
proportion to his diligent use of natural
· means, that St. Aloysius acquired, after a
time, and with some difficulty no doubt, such
a spirit of prayer, such a power of thinking,
that his thoughts were so completely under
his own control that he was entire master of
them, he ruled them, not they him, as is too
often the way with us. Now why should we
not strive that our lives may be lives of
prayer, pure and beautiful before God, as his
was ? Why is it there is so little of the spirit
of prayer in us ? As we have already said, it
is in great measure because of our selfishness,
our supineness, our want of recollection ; but
it would be worth trying to acquire it if only
for our own sakes, our own peace of mind, our
own happiness and content. Our Mother is
so willing to help her own if only they would
allow her. She would lead by the hand those
who are yet but novices in prayer; she would

show them the best way of praying; she would teach them what to say to endear themselves to the Heart of God.

As it is, how often it happens that when we set about our morning meditation, or pray at other times, we are so distracted, and have so little power of control over our thoughts, that we leave it. Instead of peaceful content, willingness to suffer for God, determination to fulfil His will by persevering in prayer, and to bear patiently whatever He may appoint, whether it be dryness and aridity, or consolation, we leave off our prayer, sad, uncomfortable, restless, uneasy, not loving God or our neighbour any more, of course, from such intercourse with God as this, but rather out of sorts both with God and our neighbour. Let us, then, find out the cause of this sad failure. Do we set about our prayer in a proper spirit, whether it be mental prayer or vocal, in the church or at home? Of course our prayer must be a failure and a burden, if it be not enlivened by a right intention, and animated by a right spirit. Let us learn from Mary. What was the spirit with which she went to prayer? First, and before all else, it was to adore her God, to pay Him the worship she owed Him, to do on earth what the blessed are doing in heaven,—adore, love, praise, and

thank the great, the good God. We sometimes barely think of this at all as we scram-
ble through our prayers in an unseemly
manner. There is often no spirit of adoration in our prayers at all, nor in the long
vocal prayers some people are in the habit of
*reading*, for we can hardly call it praying.
Is it at all like prayer, this reading as we
would read any pious book of instruction?
Is it performed in the spirit of prayer, which
is the raising up of our minds and hearts to
God? Is it from the heart? and what is
prayer worth that is not from the heart? If
so, well and good; the more of such reading
the better; but to judge by the fruits it is not
always so.

We will try to make our prayer from the
heart, dear Jesus, for we will make it from
the Heart of Thy Mother. What she would
have us say we will say; what she would
have us ask for that we will ask for; whatever graces that dear Mother's Heart would
entreat Thee for, these we will beg of Thee
to bestow, for she knows our needs better than
we do ourselves. But first we will ever kneel,
in lowliest humility, in silent adoration, before
our God, who faith teaches us is bending an
attentive ear to our prayer, listening graciously to our words. How should we not

love Him if we could see Him. Let us strive
to bring Him to our minds, let us picture
Him to our imagination, the good God, all
attention to our words, loving to hear us
speak, and listening far more lovingly than we
sometimes see a fond parent listening to the
lispings of a beloved child.

Go, then, and lisp out your prayers to God;
fulfil first your duty to your Creator, by
adoring, and praising, and thanking Him;
then perhaps His goodness may invite you
to a delightful familiarity. But ever, and
before all, go to God in the company of Mary
your Mother; let her present your prayers;
attend at Mass with her; receive Holy Communion with her; so will you please God and
render your prayer acceptable in His sight,
for if you go to prayer in the company of
Mary, with her dispositions and intentions
offered to God as your own, you will never go
unprepared, and thus be "as one who
tempteth God." We are told we never go
into the church without coming away either
better or worse than we were; and it would
be a pity, to say the least, to spend those
precious moments to no purpose. When we
go to the church to pray, let us really pray,
let us worship our God, who is truly present
there, with our whole hearts, our whole souls,

and our whole minds. Let us worship Him
likewise while about our work, in a quiet,
simple, loving way, doing perfectly whatever
we are about, working in the presence of God
by a constant offering of whatever we are
doing, by little compacts with God, as for
instance, offering our work for this or that
intention, by the thousand and one ways love
will suggest when the Mother of fair love has
really possession of her child, when her spirit
really influences the soul that is wholly her
own, when that soul, possessed by Mary, lives
and grows under her fostering care, and ceases
entirely to live for itself, but is bent upon
serving God and God alone, whom it finds so
easily, whom it learns to love so devotedly,
to whom it becomes united so closely and
happily by the sweet way of Mary, and
with whom it holds such happy converse by
the prayer it has learned from the Heart
of Mary.

Yes, if we have rightly thought of the
various loves of the Heart of Mary, or rather
of some of them, we shall pray in harmony
with these loves; we shall pour out our soul
in love for God the Father, Son, and Holy
Ghost; we shall find our hearts beat in uni-
son with the Sacred Heart of Jesus; we shall
bathe our souls in the Precious Blood that

Sacred Heart contains; we shall adore our hidden Lord and Lover in the tabernacle; we shall take Him to our hearts in Holy Communion: all this we will do in union with the Heart of Mary. We will worship the whole court of Heaven; we will love those blessed ones, and strive to resemble them on earth by our songs of praise, our constant prayer of thanksgiving. Yes, we will love and join, as best we may on earth, in the hymns of the Angels in heaven. We will love, too, and thank God for, the goodness of the just on earth, and rejoice in the glory they give our God. We will love the poor sinners who are being led away from their allegiance to their Creator, we will win them back by our prayer of love, by a prayer from the Heart of Mary, that earnest, ardent, imploring prayer of impetration that God loves to hear, and that He surely listens to. This will thy children do, sweet Mother, by the grace thou wilt obtain for them; we will love all God's creatures, all mankind, and save them by our love, which shall follow them on to dear Purgatory, where we hope to bring many by the prayer of Mary, that we have offered for them, thus saving them from a fate that it is impossible for the human mind to meditate on without horror, or without striving with every energy the good God has given us to avert, if it lie in our power to do so, and we know it does, for the word of God has said: "Pray for one another, that you may be saved : for the continual prayer of a just man availeth much. He who causeth a sinner to be converted from the error of his ways, shall save his soul from death."—*St. James* v., 16-20.

Sweet Mother, now with child-like love we cluster at thy feet, begging of thee that, having thought of thy love, the flame it has enkindled in our hearts may never flicker or fade away, but that, burning brightly all through our lives, it may be found still brightly burning at the moment of our death, that precious moment when Jesus will come to claim His own, for thine own are His, O Mary, none more truly so. We trust, sweet Mother, that with thy help, when the time arrives for our souls to leave our bodies and appear before God, we shall look fearlessly into our dear Lord's face, and see that it is smiling upon us, and that because we loved on earth we shall then be eternally loved by the God of love in heaven. May God in His mercy grant that it be so with us ; may death in that dread moment of our departure from this life find us with the lamp of love lit by Mary's own hands burning brightly, and enabling us to endure the trial, waiting as it were happily for God to claim His own, which we truly are, since, sweet Mother, may His Holy Spirit be praised, we are wholly thine.

# ADDITIONAL MEDITATIONS.

### I.

#### The Love of our Lady for her own.

Do we understand the love of possession? Doubtless. It soon springs up in the mind of the child, and grows with its growth. It is not an evil when the possession is just, unless carried to excess. The child loves to possess its toys; the lover sighs to possess the one he loves; the bridegroom rejoices in the possession of his bride; the mother in the possession of her child; and our Mother in heaven rejoices in the possession of her own. Her little earthly flock is a great delight to the heavenly shepherdess, a great joy. If we know this, if we feel it, are we who rejoice in the name of Mary's own striving to increase our Mother's joy, by giving her more children, by adding to her flock? We ourselves feel the beauty of the " True Devotion;" we feel how secure are those who embrace it and

10

perseveringly practise it; we know how well armed they are for the conflict of this life; we feel sure they will most certainly reach heaven, that if they do not stray from the path of Mary its last step is into heaven. We know all this. We picture our Mother in heaven, speaking to her children on earth, as she sends them forth to work for her. "Fear not, little flock, for it has pleased your Heavenly Father to give you a kingdom." We believe that our Lady blesses with special blessing those who are her own. And yet, are we striving to extend her kingdom? Are we adding to Mary's flock one little lamb after another? Are we striving with might and main to hasten the coming of that time which saints, the lovers of Mary, tell us is surely to come, "the age of Mary," that time when Jesus will reign in all hearts, because Mary will have established her reign in all hearts? Are we letting our light shine before men, or are we hiding it under a bushel? Are we calling our friends and neighbours to rejoice with us in the treasure we have found, or are we standing idle when there is so much work to be done? "The harvest indeed is great, but the labourers are few." Mary's harvest, Mary's children must gather together from the east and the west; they must band

together; they must ever have one thought,
how best they may help to establish the
kingdom of God upon earth, by planting the
good seed of true devotion to Mary. The
work can be done in so many ways: by lending
a book, by a few words spoken along with a
silent prayer, by persevering efforts in some
cases where, strange to say, there exists
prejudice against the devotion. Love will
teach us, if we are truly her loving, devoted
children, how to bend those around to the
sweet empire of Mary, until Mary possesses
really, far more completely than at present,
her rightful place in Christ's Church as its
Mother. Mother of our Lord, the Head of the
Church, she must of necessity be Mother of
His mystical body the Church. "Behold thy
Mother," spoke Jesus from His cross. Why
do not Mary's children petition the Vicar of
Christ to proclaim to the nations from the
cross, where our Lord's love of him and his
love of his Lord have placed him, to proclaim,
I say, in union with his Master, "Behold thy
Mother," by consecrating the Church to the
Maternal Heart of Mary?

We need special help at special times; we
need to throw ourselves upon Mary's maternal
care if we would escape shipwreck in these
stormy times. Holy Angels, whisper to your

clients to trust themselves to Mary, to consecrate themselves entirely to her, to hope in
her, to love her as their very own most precious Mother. "Powerful as an army set in
battle array," she will defend us from our
enemies, she will intercede, she will protect,
she will guard as most precious treasures all
that are devotedly given to her. Mothers,
bring your children, and give them to Mary;
teach them while young the sweet way of
Mary; so will you bring them to their home
in heaven. Pray for those you love, that they
may learn this most sweet, safe, secure way
to God. Thus will families, united together
on earth, be united together in heaven; thus,
too, will pastor and people stand before the
judgment seat of God in exceeding joy.
Happy are those pastors who have confided
their flocks to the maternal care of Mary,
and consecrated them to her, and taught
them how themselves to ratify this consecration. Thus can pastors imitate mothers,
who bring their children to be baptized
before they have reason to understand what
is being done for them, and then see that
they are taught when they are capable of
understanding. We most of us enter this
sweet way of Mary not fully understanding
what it implies, trusting to those who have

gone before us; but if we persevere, soon,
like the dawning of the morning, will appear
the wondrous rays of liberty and light, leading
the soul into a new life, opening hidden things
to view, revealing to us our God as we never
before knew Him, for truly Mary makes us
know Him in some degree, though it be but
little, as she knew Him on earth.

Well will it be for us if we enter on this
way; well for us if we lead all we can therein;
well indeed will it be if we persevere, and do
not stray therefrom when once we have
entered it; for this we may do through carelessness, through want of watchfulness, through
negligence. We can, if we choose, advance,
and then retrace our steps, for it is with this
devotion as with all else in this world, it depends entirely on our own correspondence
with grace whether we reap its advantages or
not. We may be drawn into close union with
Jesus by faithfully keeping in Mary's company, and then we may gradually relax, grow
cold, and lose our hold of the Hand of Jesus,
which was leading and supporting us, and
with tears may try in vain to recover again its
warm clasp, that is, the almost sensible perception of His merciful guidance and support,
until our Mother in pity comes to help us, and
shows us how we have strayed from our path,

and leads us on our road again to Jesus's feet.
Look well, then, and examine, you who belong
to Mary. Are you doing your best for your
Mother? Are you doing your best in your
own soul, your best in the souls of others, or
are you lagging on the way? Stir yourself
up if it be so, rouse yourself to greater vigi-
lance, to more earnestness; commence again
your practices of devotion with renewed
vigour; remember the constant little acts by
which you repeat again and again to our Lady
during the day that you renounce your own
spirit, your own will, that you may live by
her spirit, by her will, and that you do whatever you do because you believe that she
would wish you to do it, not because you
yourself wish it. This devotion, I repeat it,
contains and will lead to all perfection : this
is living a life most pleasing to our God ; this
is indeed being cast in the mould of Mary, to
be formed anew, to live no longer by your own
spirit, but by the sweet spirit of Jesus and
Mary ; for all Mary lived for was to fulfil the
will of Jesus. She had none of her own
apart from Him, and so it should be with us,
a total subduing and renunciation of self, that
"God alone" may be our motto, His holy
Mother's honour our pass-word, the love of
one another our daily practice. As the angels

and saints, God's heavenly children, love one
another, so let us, looking upon ourselves and
others as God's earthly children, as in truth
we are, act as God's children should, and love
one another. Let us begin during this month
of May. Bless thy children, Mother Mary,
that they may live as thou didst, a life of
love, such as may show them to be true
children of the God of love. Amen, amen.

## II.

### Our Lady's Love of Virginity.

Our Blessed Lady has been set on high,
conspicuous to all the world and to all ages,
as the VIRGIN Mother and pattern of virginity,
shining brightly as the spotless Virgin, as
Mary, Queen of Virgins, as Mary the great
lover of virginity. Mary, our Mother, our
own sweet Mother, loved by God for thy love
and choice of virginity, make thy children to
love it too. Obtain for them light from the
Holy Ghost, thy Heavenly Spouse, that may
reveal to them the beauty of this virtue.
Thou didst prefer this virtue to the great
happiness of being Mother of God. What
then must be its value in thy eyes, and if in

thine, in God's eyes also, for thou didst only
view things as God views them.  Was it not
this virtue which set thee apart, and consecrated thee so entirely to God? thou wast
not connected with aught of this earth except
in God and for God; thou, above all others,
saints and prophets, wert pure and separate
from all earthly things; apart from God there
was no link, no tie which in any way connected thee with them; even thy dear Spouse
St. Joseph would never have enjoyed that
privilege if he had not been chosen the Foster Father of God, thy Son.    Thou didst
receive nought from this earth which could
make thee what thou art, though thou gavest
to the earth its Saviour, and in this thou art
like to God.    God is virginal and fruitful,
and so is Mary His chosen one; in this, as in
all things else, does she resemble Him, so
perfectly does she reflect her Maker and her
God.

As she was herself, so she loves her children to be, so far as they are able; therefore
does she love the virgins of the earth, and
longs that they who are capable of living
thus on earth should embrace this holy state.
Most dear are they to this sweet Mother;
they know not themselves the special love
the Virgin of all virgins has for those who are

imitating herself in this virtue, those I mean who truly love it, who appreciate it, who perfectly practise it. We shall never know until we come to heaven the greatness of this virtue, and perhaps it is well for some that they do not know it, it might raise a vain complacency in them. Doubtless, also, it is well for many that they have not embraced this holy state. Matrimony, too, is holy, and many persons could not save their souls except in a state of matrimony. The married life, though inferior, has especial advantages for sanctification; patience, forbearance, charity, and, above all, humility, are among its fruits,—and virginity without humility is nothing worth in God's sight. Better be humble and married, than a virgin and proud. But Mary's own will please God by being lowly, humble virgins, most dear to their Mother. They will be God's virgins, receiving ever from God, and giving ever of their abundance to others. They will keep aloof from all of this earth as far as duty will permit, receiving nothing from it beyond what is necessary to enable them to serve God, loving nothing of it, having no pleasure from earthly things, loving only the things of heaven, striving to preserve themselves pure for the sake of the All-Holy, All-Pure God.

" The prayer of the humble (and therefore pure) soul pierceth the clouds."

If we could but see our pure, holy Mother in Heaven, as she watches some favoured children of hers on earth; if we could but understand the love which fills her sweet Heart for chaste souls, dove-like souls, who are on this earth but not of it, beautiful because shining with a lustre borrowed from Heaven; who are wrapt in the arms of God so closely, so happily, even in this world; who can hear God's whispers, for His peace is in their hearts,—I say, if we could but see and understand this, as we may by faith, how highly should we prize this holy state. Their Mother, the Queen in Heaven, rejoices with such souls; she carefully watches over them that they may not tarnish the bright lustre which makes them so lovely in God's sight, for that Mother knows well what we are apt so quickly to forget, the sad facility with which we can tarnish the purity of our souls. Some have compared it to the ease with which a beautiful mirror of purest crystal can be tarnished by even a faint breath. Those who live in Mary's company learn from her how to preserve their souls fresh, fragrant to God, as flowers of earth well-pleasing to Him. Close to the

chaste soul and Heart of Mary, they learn
their Mother's love of virginity, they feel,
they think what they could not put into
words; they look into the face of the Immaculate Virgin, with its fair virginity imprinted on it, the sweet, loving eyes with that
indescribable, that Mary-like look which we
so love to picture to our minds; this they do,
and so draw nearer and nearer to their Queen,
and Mary whispers in their hearts sweet
thoughts about God's love of purity. She
speaks to them about the beautiful virgin
Saints who have lived on earth. She brings
to mind perhaps some whom they may know,
whom they have themselves seen with the
freshness of innocent virginity beaming so
softly on their faces like the gentle dawn;
and thus they learn to love this virtue more
and more, and they thank God for those to
whom He has given grace to embrace this
state. If we are happily virgins ourselves, we
will thank God from our hearts, and prize the
great gift God gave us in permitting us to be
so. We will use all the means we can to
preserve this precious gift. We will strive to
remain detached from all of this earth,—we
will be humble, mortified, unselfish, seeking
only the things of God, chaste, pure, pleasing,
beloved by Him, as most dear children, raised

by His grace above all the things of earth, on this earth but not of it, living in this world but not loving it, loving only God and the things of God, looking up to the Home of Love in Heaven, where those who have not clung to the joys of life in time, shall have a special joy in the eternal life to come.

"My beloved to me, and I to Him, Who feedeth amongst the lilies."

## III.

## The Love of the Heart of our Lady for Christian Parents.

In the Heart of our Lady there is a specially tender love, which has a distinct character of its own, for Christian parents and Christian homes. God has a special love for, and gives a special help to fathers and mothers, gives indeed the grand grace of a special sacrament to enable them to fulfil their high office. How could it be otherwise? Parents are in some sense the instruments (as they may be called the occasional causes) which God uses in His great work of creating human souls, the souls He so loves, the souls that are so intensely dear to Him. God's loves are

our Lady's loves. She too loves you, dear
Christian parents, you know not how dearly,
how earnestly; she sees so much you do not
see; she sees such wonderful things in your
vocation which you perhaps have never seen
or imagined. There is so much that is great
and noble in your state of life, and resulting
from it, that our Lady sees and knows, but
which you never thought of when you entered
it. Our Lady will show something of them to
you, she will at least give you a higher idea
of your state if you will allow her. You may
have entered upon it simply from human
motives. You may have had little thought
of the noble office you had to discharge for
your God, the grand work He had entrusted
to you; but it is not yet too late to remedy
this negligence. Give yourselves and your
families to the care of Mary, consecrate all to
her Maternal Heart, and learn from it the
love she has for you and yours, her maternal
solicitude, her desire that you should be such
parents as God intended you to be, that you
should resemble Him, imitate Him in the
especial way your office enables you to do.
We have said elsewhere that every Christian
household should in some respect resemble
the household of Nazareth. There is the
father who should resemble the dear St.

Joseph, the good, the just; there is the mother who should be copying in her daily life, in the performance of all her duties, the Mother above all mothers; there is a little infant in most households, and how often have we not had a good thought put into our minds, a thought of Jesus and Mary, by seeing a pure, holy mother bending over the little one in her arms.

Sit and meditate upon this; it will be good and profitable for you, and there will rise up before you thoughts you could hardly put into words. There is the parent's office adumbrating that of God Himself. There is the father seeming, with all reverence be it said, in an indistinct, shadowy way to bring to our minds the Eternal Father. There is the mother imitating her God by her fruitfulness. But such thoughts are to be pondered in the mind rather than put down in writing. Let parents meditate long and lovingly upon the grand office, the great dignity they have in being parents. Let them resolve to do all that lies in their power to perform their office well, and resolve to look upon their state in the light of that love with which the Mother of fair love regards it. Let parents resolve to make their homes homes of love, where the God of love shall dwell; let them resolve to

do all in their power to guard the gifts God
bestows upon them, remembering that their
children are God's children, that they belong
more to Him than to themselves; let them
reflect that if a king or queen entrusted their
children to them to guard, what care they
would take of the precious charge, both because of the honour and the reward. Therefore let parents entrusted with the care of
immortal souls, God's children, consider that
they are honoured by God in this life, and
that a very great reward is in store for them
in the next if they shall have reared their
children, God's children, according to the will
and wish of God. Happy day to be looked
forward to, when parents and children stand
together before God to receive their sentence.
Happy parents who can then in joy and glad
delight look up to your Divine Master and
exclaim, " I am here, O Lord, with those
whom Thou hast given me." Happy parents,
who so labour to perform your duties in this
short day of mercy and of time, that on that
grand day of justice and eternity you may be
able to say, as you kneel at the feet of Jesus,
and meet His sweet look of recompensing
love, " And of those whom Thou hast given to
me I have not lost one." May it be so. May
the hope that it may be so encourage you in

your labours and sufferings, and spur you on
to still greater efforts to save the souls of
those whom the sweet Saviour of souls has
given you to save for Him, whom the dear
Mother of mercy desires so to see safe in
the home above, which we can only enter by
suffering and sacrifice for ourselves and
others, by performing the particular work
or mission for which our God created us.

233

# APPENDIX.

It being customary, in books written for the Month of May, to add examples, prayers, and practices, to the chapter read, we have added this Appendix, in which something may be found useful in this way. As some of the readings for each day are rather short, the reader can lengthen them by the addition of some portion of the following.

## I.

The Blessed Trinity is the beginning and the end of every devotion we practise, of every good work we perform. Our whole lives should be one continued worship of the Ever-Blessed and Adorable Trinity. If in the past this Adorable Mystery, this wonderful revelation of faith, has not been revered as it should be, if it has not had the place in our thoughts and actions it should have had, this Month of May we will commence, this very

day we will strive to gain a great spirit of
adoration. Father Faber tells us how the
Church cries out on Trinity Sunday in child-
like wonder, "O Beata Trinitas, O Beata
Trinitas." We will throughout this day join
with the Immaculate Heart of Mary and the
Holy Angels in some short prayer or as-
piration, some act of adoration of the Ever-
Adorable Trinity. The Angels repeat the
same words over and over again, let us do the
same; while going about our work let our
hearts be echoing the eternal "Sanctus,
Sanctus, Sanctus," of the Angels in heaven.

## II.

Our Father who art in heaven. We will
repeat this over and over again during the
day. We will say it as if with Mary's lips;
we will offer it as it was said by the lips of
Jesus; we will linger over the words, pondering them, and they will grow sweeter and
sweeter to us. Our Father, our own Father,
the Father of Jesus and Mary. The Father of
the Eternal Word, the Father who loves us so
greatly, the Father who so desires, who so
deserves that we should trust Him as loving
children. We will think whether in the past
we have trusted Him as we should have done.

If we find that we have been wanting in this virtue of hope, that we have been distrustful, which is a great sign of a cold heart and a weak faith, we will resolve to be so no longer. We will begin at once to practise this most necessary virtue, to stifle in our breasts every thought that is contrary to it, and this will endear us to our Heavenly Father. If we do not practise hope here we can never practise it hereafter; though its seed is from heaven and its root is in heaven, yet it springs up and blossoms only on an earthly soil, and is of great beauty and most pleasing to our God.

"He will have mercy on us, according to our trust in Him." We will then make frequent acts of hope this day, in union with the Mother of holy Hope.

## III.

The unruffled repose of the Son in the Bosom of the Eternal Father. O Eternal Word, we long to see that Beatific Vision, the Word in the Bosom of His Father, but though we may not see it here, we rejoice in the thought of it. We may and we should be glad and joyful at the thought of God's joy. "Delight in the Lord, and He will give thee the desires of thy heart." Truly

God loves the cheerful giver, the grateful child of grace, ever pleased with its God, ever praising Him, ever rejoicing in Him. Have we done this in the past? Have we thanked God for His own great glory as we should have done? Have our souls magnified our God as Mary's did? Have our spirits rejoiced in God our Saviour? If not, let us at least begin now at once, for those who truly love rejoice in God and praise Him. Let us think to-day of some words that will remind us that we are this day to praise our God, to rejoice in Him, to love Him with Mary's Heart, and therefore to delight in Him and be glad.

" Sing joyfully to God all the earth; serve ye the Lord with gladness.

" Come in before His presence with exceeding great joy.

" Know ye that the Lord He is God; He made us, and not we ourselves.

" We are His people, and the sheep of His pasture.

" Go ye into His gates with praise, into His courts with hymns, and give glory to Him.

" Praise ye His name, for the Lord is sweet: His mercy endureth for ever, and His

truth to generation and generation. Glory,
&c."—*Psalm* xcix.

## IV.

"The Spirit of God filleth the whole earth."
Have we in the past been sufficiently devout
to the Holy Ghost? Have we thought sufficiently of the office of the Holy Ghost?
Have we considered that we ourselves are the
temples of the Holy Ghost, that He dwells
within us. Good God, little indeed do we
think of this, or we should have a far greater
respect for ourselves than we have, as being
what in truth we are, " temples of the living
God ;" we should reverence ourselves as the
sanctuaries of God : we should be careful to
avoid whatever might ruffle His repose within
us ; we should live in God's Spirit, and we
should be ever striving to mortify and subdue
our own selfish spirit ; we should live in
charity, joy, peace, and patience ; we should,
in one word, be most dear children of Mary.
Pray now for a great devotion to the Holy
Ghost, and practise it constantly. Learn the
beautiful hymns to the Holy Ghost, and recite
them often during the day as you go about
your work, and especially at the commencement of the day, to invoke God's blessing

upon it, and you will find how far more smoothly those days will pass that are lived in the sunshine of God's Holy Spirit.

## V.

We will resolve to make some special visits in honour of the Precious Blood, which our faith teaches us is present in the Sacred Host, the Blessed Sacrament. In receiving Holy Communion we will make acts of faith in the great truth that we have then within us the same Precious Blood which was shed for us on Calvary. We will adore it, we will bow down in spirit before it, and offer the adoration of the angels as it lay in the streets of Jerusalem; we will make reparation for the outrages and insults offered to it; we will love it in union with the Heart of Mary. During the busy hours of the day we will from time to time turn our thoughts to the silent church, visit it in spirit, and unite our worship with that of the adoring angels there clustered round the Precious Blood. When present at Benediction we will offer it to thank our God for this earth's treasure, this unspeakable treasure that we children of earth possess, the Precious Blood of Jesus. Eternal Father, I offer Thee the Precious Blood of Jesus, in satisfaction for my sins, and the wants of holy Church.

"Eternal Father, we offer Thee the Precious Blood of Jesus shed for us with such great love and bitter pain from His Right Hand, and through the merits and the efficacy of that Blood we entreat Thy Divine Majesty to grant us Thy holy benediction in order that we may be defended thereby from all our enemies, and set free from every ill, whilst we say, Benedictio Dei omnipotentis, Patris et Filii et Spiritus Sancti, descendat super nos et maneat semper. Amen."* Pater Noster, Ave Maria, Gloria, in thanksgiving.


## VI.

Make a practice of constantly asking what you require through the Sacred Heart. If in great need, if tempted to impatience, for instance, say quickly, "Patience of the Heart of Jesus, make me patient;" or if in doubt what it is best for you to do in any matter, "Providence of the Heart of Jesus, direct me,"† and so on. The constant habit of ejaculatory prayer is very useful to the soul

* Indulgenced.  † Mère Marie de la Providence.

in life, and also when death shall come. Those who have had this habit in life will find, when brought near death, that it is of the greatest help and comfort to them, and that they are reciting constantly in their hearts, when unable to do so with their lips, little prayers invoking the sweet names of Jesus and Mary.

## VII.

Repeat during the day, every hour or oftener, that sweet powerful invocation, "Corpus Domini Nostri Jesu Christi, custodiat animam meam in vitam æternam. Amen." It is a beautiful prayer, and a most efficacious one. Well for us will it be if we make constant use of it; holy shall we become, holy in thought, word, and deed; pure and bright will our souls gleam in God's sight, strengthened by the Body and Blood of God, that we shall really receive in a spiritual manner by means of this prayer. Let us commence this happy habit at once; it will bring untold blessings with .it; it will brighten and invigorate our whole lives.

## VIII.

Strive to acquire a habit of making spiritual visits to the Blessed Sacrament when you are not able to visit it otherwise. Go with your soul when your body is not able. Our soul is a spirit,—we can go in spirit to heaven itself. Likewise, when making a journey, visit in spirit the lonely tabernacles of the towns you pass, where Jesus is, and where He is left so many long hours alone. Make a resolution that you will live close to the Blessed Sacrament when it is possible for you to do so; that you will put yourself to some inconvenience to do so, and choose rather to lose some of this world's goods or conveniences than to live at a distance from this Treasure of the earth.

## IX.

Let us honour St. Michael by constantly reminding him of his great happiness in standing firm in the hour of temptation. It will be a great help to us in our own temptation, for this grand archangel will gratefully acknowledge our devotion by fighting for us in our temptations. And how much do we

11

need help, how weak we are in temptation, how often we yield, how often do we give way to the suggestions of the enemy of souls, how we risk our eternity of happiness. What if that grand archangel had given way at that momentous crisis of his existence. How horrified we feel at the thought of that beautiful spirit, that bright angel we so love, falling, being changed into a devil. Let us apply this thought to ourselves; let us pray that we may be brave in temptation; let us pray to St. Michael to help us in our fight with the devil, the world, and the flesh.

Strive to acquire the custom they have in some Catholic countries of saluting the angels upon entering a room before you salute the people who are in it. This can, of course, be done secretly and without making oneself noticed in the least. In the midst of a conversation also it is useful to salute the guardian angel of the person you are speaking to. The habit will become easy after a time, and will be a most useful one.

Mary, Queen of Angels, pray for us.

## X.

Let us honour the dear St. Joseph by offering the Heart of Jesus in thanksgiving for the graces bestowed upon him, and for the increase of his glory. Let us strive to imitate his hidden goodness, his quiet way of working; let us resolve to avoid ostentation in our works; let us love little acts of virtue, secrets between our soul and God.

## XI.

The saints were, after all, human beings, though we sometimes almost think of them as though they were of a different nature from our own; but it is not so; they simply lived a real life, and by real we mean that they lived more in the midst of the realities of faith, they realized the truths of faith, they lived more in the supernatural than in the natural life, they knew well that the things we see are not so real, not so true as the things we do not see. Let us strive to imitate them, let our conversation be in heaven, let us make friends with the angels and saints; thus shall we be able to do as they did, and endear ourselves to God as they did.

## XII.

When we are in temptation let us pray for poor sinners in similar temptations, those who are in danger of yielding to temptation, those who have given way and are steeped in sin. This will be a most efficacious prayer for ourselves and others too; it will be a pure, unselfish prayer, most pleasing to God. When we are in temptation we are too often very selfish, we lose very much of the merit of the combat by being wrapt up in ourselves instead of generously throwing ourselves out upon others in that most trying time, which is best met by unselfish acts of charity to others. We may have prayed for others, we may have longed to save poor sinners, but when the time came to suffer for them we have drawn back. The time of temptation is a time of great suffering; the racking of the soul is far worse than the racking of the body. God help us in that hour. He will assuredly help those who are striving with might and main to help others.

## XIII.

Resolve to make the Stations of the Way of the Cross whenever you can, in order to obtain for the holy souls the wonderful indulgences attached to this devotion. It will take but little time. If you live near a church where the Stations are formally erected you can go from station to station with a little act of love and sorrow at each. Any little prayer said at each with devotion, suffices to gain the many plenary indulgences, provided that the person saying it meditate according to his ability on the Passion of our Lord Jesus Christ. Those who are ill, or do not live where the Stations are erected, may procure a crucifix indulgenced for them from some priest who has the power, and by reciting fourteen Paters and Aves, and at the end of these other five Paters, and five Aves, and five Glorias, and again one Pater, Ave, and Gloria for the Pope, "holding in their hands all the while a brass crucifix" which has been blessed by one who has faculties for the purpose, will gain the same indulgences as though they made the Stations in the church.

Beads blessed by the Canons Regular of the Holy Cross have the Indulgence of 500 days for each Hail Mary and Our Father said on such beads. The Indulgence is applicable to the Souls in Purgatory. It is not necessary to say a Rosary, the Indulgence can be gained as often as one says one single Our Father, or Hail Mary.*

## XIV.

Let us remind St. Peter often of the great grace accorded him, that best of all graces, the grace of contrition. Let us remind him of those tears that so eased his soul, those contrite tears that brought him peace. Let us beseech him to obtain such for us. He denied his Lord after but one communion; we have denied our Lord, we have driven Him from us perhaps after many communions; " we have denied by our conduct that we ever knew Him."

---

* The power of blessing Beads to the effect of gain-ing the above-mentioned Indulgence was given to the General of the Order of the Canons Regular of the Holy Cross, by Leo X., on August 20th, 1516. Pope Pius IX., on January 9th, 1848, authorized the General of the Order to delegate the power given to him by Leo X. to every priest of the Order. In England, address to the Rev. Joseph Van den Dries, Canon Regular of the Holy Cross, the Presbytery, New-market, Cambridgeshire.

## XV.

Let us learn from St. John "love for the brethren," let us beseech for ourselves and others the great grace of fraternal charity. We see sad sights now-a-days arising from want of unity of our dear Lord's members one with another,—rash judgment in a grievous degree, uncharitable words written as well as spoken. Let us strive to renew amongst Catholics the true Catholic spirit of unity. I do not mean unity as regards matters of faith, —thank God we have that,—but unity upon other points, or on one point, viz., a great unity of love one for another. It should be a real pain to one Catholic to hear another spoken against. Let us strive to make ourselves very dear, specially dear, specially beloved by Jesus, on account of our great love for one another. "This is My commandment, that you love one another." "By this shall all men know that you are My disciples, if you have love one for another."

## XVI.

We will resolve to show our love for our Holy Father by our love and reverence for his representatives. Many members of Christ's Church may never have the happiness of knowing the Holy Father, of personally paying their homage to him; but all may honour their bishops, and respect them, and pray for them. This is a duty, but it is a much-neglected duty. If we have been negligent hitherto in this matter, let us commence at once. We lose many graces ourselves by not impetrating grace for those who guide us.

## XVII.

Let us think more often upon the great favour vouchsafed us in being members of Christ's Church; let us thank God for this precious gift we possess, the gift of faith; let us have apostles' hearts, to bring others into the Church. If we are really close to Mary's Heart she will implant within us her own desire to convert others to the truth. We will be Mary's apostles. It is but giving Jesus the desires of His Heart when we give Him Mary's desires. She but reflects Him.

Not to the apostles alone was it said, "Go and teach all nations," for every one must be an apostle, at least by example and by prayer. But we need not go far away to evangelize the nations, our own nation is here. Let us convert that first; let us give Mary back her dower. If we are really in earnest we shall find many ways of contributing to this grand work, as, for example, taking a friend to church, and thus bringing him to our Lord's feet, and asking Him to bless him; lending a book; saying a chance word, with a silent prayer that God will bless it; and so on *ad libitum*. O Mary, convert England; teach us how we may help thee to bring thy erring children back to the bosom of Mother Church.

## XVIII.

Let us pray for priests; it is our dear Lord's wish; it is one special object for prayer He has placed before us: "The harvest indeed is great, but the labourers are few. Pray ye therefore the Lord of the harvest that He send forth *labourers* into His harvest."

The priest can bless wherever he goes, the priest can do untold good. Let us venerate them, let us assist them, let us minister to them, let us constantly bring to our minds the words that seem sometimes forgotten by Catholics, " He that heareth you heareth Me ; he that despiseth you despiseth Me."

## XIX.

Let us resolve to offer constantly in intention all the Masses that are being said in different parts of the world. We may often want to pray for some special intention, but our occupations may hinder our applying our minds to prayer as we would wish. Let us then join our work to the Mass being offered ; let us offer it to God, in union with our Lord, for the special intention, whatever it may be ; let us thus join in spirit, and we shall reap much grace. Before composing ourselves to sleep, let us make an offering of all the Masses that will be said during the night in other parts of the world. Let us ask our guardian angel to assist at them for us, and to be asking graces, and thanking and praising God for us during the time of our rest.

## XX.

We all know how weak we are. If we do not, so much the worse for us. We are indeed weak, we need all the grace we can get. How is it, then, we neglect that great grace of graces, Holy Communion? Ah, it is an evil that cannot be sufficiently deplored, the prevailing neglect of Holy Communion. By no other act can we give God the glory which we can give Him by Holy Communion. And is it not indeed sad that God should be deprived of the glory we might so easily give Him if we would but go frequently and devoutly to Holy Communion? And as regards our own souls, we can receive in Holy Communion graces such as we can receive at no other time, and in no other way. We can be raised above ourselves, we can surmount all difficulties, we can keep our souls in peace in the midst of the greatest sufferings, by the help Holy Communion will give us, and when unavoidably deprived of this Heavenly Food let us make many and fervent spiritual communions.

## XXI.

What a good work it would be to enable some ardent soul to enter religion, and consecrate itself to God. How many young girls there are, truly pious, humble, and with good natural abilities, longing to be the spouses of Jesus, but who, having no money, are unable to enter a religious order, where they might satisfy their wish to belong entirely to Jesus, and where they might be the means of saving very many souls. It would indeed be a happy and consoling thought for persons on their death-beds to think that they had provided for a spouse of Jesus, and that in consequence they enjoyed the great blessing and advantage of having the prayers of the whole community offered for them as for a benefactor. This is a work of charity by no means common. I have only known it practised once. May God bless the good man who had the charity to do it. I pray God that many others may follow his example. Religious orders work hard for the spiritual, some also for the temporal, good of others. They pray and work for the world, and the world in return should help to support them. All should try to do something in this way. Sometimes a community of religious is established in a place, and the Catholic people of that place do not seem to consider it their duty to assist them to the best of their power. Sometimes a community is decried because its members are forced to go out and personally solicit alms for their necessary support, and yet it is not taken into consideration that those good sisters are giving their services gratis for the good of others, either by teaching or nursing. I know one community where there are six sisters engaged in teaching, who receive no salary whatever, and where more than a dozen sisters are engaged amongst the poor, in mission work, instructing them, and nursing their sick night and day, and yet, when reluctantly, in order to avoid breaking their rules by getting into debt, they went out to beg, great was the outcry raised by even some good people against them. Is this fair? It may offend the eyes of respectable and pious people to see religious going from house to house begging. It is certainly a most unpleasant business, as the poor sisters know too well; but will those who censure do a little to save them from it, by personally exerting themselves, or depriving themselves of something to prevent its being done? Resolve to assist some communities for the love of Jesus, if only by collecting pence on cards for them.

## XXII.

Holy Mother, we implore thee, by thy purity, by thy love of virtue, by thy Immaculate Conception, by thy sinlessness, thy spotlessness, show us how we may keep clear of sin, how we may preserve our souls unstained. It would be well to think, in the midst of our many works, " Are we striving to keep our souls from sin, from venial sin?" Ah, what a pity it is that we so mix up the nasty matter of venial sin with our good actions, though we know very well that ten hundred years of good works would not of themselves alone atone for one venial sin. Nothing but the sufferings of Jesus could do that. Let our great object in life be to avoid venial sin, to hinder it in ourselves and others, and much shall we do by this to extend God's kingdom on earth.

## XXIII.

"Much peace have they that love Thy law, and to them there is no stumbling-block." (Ps. cxviii. 165.) "The just hath hope in his death." (Prov. xiv. 32.) Yes, the end of one who has lived to be perfect, of one who has striven with might and main to love the God of Love, who has endeavoured to please Him in every word and work, is full of hope and peace. When the last hour arrives for that happy soul to live on earth, calmly can it rest, with a great hope of God's mercy; calmly can it await that grand interview it must have with its God. "What shall I say when God shall arise to judge?" We may well wonder what the first words will be that we shall speak to God. Let us make our lives God-like, and then with joy we shall say, "Lætatus sum in his quæ dicta sunt mihi, in domum Domini ibimus."

## XXIV.

If by telling a small untruth we could let all the souls out of purgatory, convert the whole world, or even empty hell of its unfortunate victims, if, I say, by telling a venial lie we could do all this, we might not do it. Think of this, meditate upon it, and surely there will be a greater guard over your words, a greater love of truthfulness, a greater horror of the least breach of this beautiful virtue. May we all love truth, may we pursue it, may we daily grow dearer to the All-holy God, by becoming a reflection, as it were, of His divine truthfulness, truthful in thought, word, and work; true children of the God of Truth. This will brighten our whole lives.

## XXV.

Let us resolve to imitate our Mother by comforting the sorrowful. How does she do so? By showing them the value of suffering. Let us do the same service for the many mourners we meet; let us lovingly encourage them to bear patiently their sufferings, by showing them how they endear themselves to God by so doing. If we have taught others this grand lesson, "the art of suffering well," we shall have done a good which, in its results and its effects, will never die. We shall be able to help others in suffering if we suffer well ourselves, our own patient suffering will give us the power to do this. As with all else so with this, what we possess ourselves we can give to others.

## XXVI.

Humility and patience. What rare virtues they are, even amongst Christians! Though the very mark of a Christian, a follower of Christ, they are scouted by many who call themselves Christians. Injustice is looked upon as unbearable, insufferable, even by the good. Alas, it is sad, it is such a contradiction to the teaching, to the counsels, at least, of Christ. In the early ages of the Church the heathen could tell who were Christians by their humility and patience. It was a sure mark by which they were known. It certainly could not be said to be so in these days. Let us strive to commence again this practice of patience. Let us Catholics be known as followers of the One who has said, " Learn of Me, for I am meek and humble of heart."

## XXVII.

Let us pray for grace to guide aright those whom God has placed in our care. If we are mothers, let us pray earnestly for this necessary grace, and strive to learn all we ought to know in order to perform our duties well. Many are the souls of infants that leave this world unbaptized from culpable ignorance on the part of mothers and others. Let those who have charge of children not their own, guardians, teachers, and others, be careful to do all in their power to preserve the souls of their charges from habits of sin, to help them to retain that innate fear of sin which is implanted in the soul until lost by constant commission of sin.

## XXVIII.

What a happy place a Christian home should be, and how pleasing is a holy home to the eyes of God. It is so for many reasons, and one especial reason is that a good Christian home bears some resemblance to the home at Nazareth. What an important thing it is to know how to make home happy. Let all examine and see if they are doing their best towards it; let each member of the family, father, mother, children, make it a point in their examination of conscience to see whether they are doing their duty to one another, whether they are doing their best to contribute to the general peace and happiness. A home where discord, and therefore unhappiness prevails, is a wretched school for virtue. Christian virtues cannot thrive in such an atmosphere.

## XXIX.

Let us fill up our vacant time with prayer. Only try the effect it will have on your whole life, the constant habit of returning to prayer at every spare moment. You may have missed your train, and are waiting for the next: instead of getting impatient at the seeming waste of time, sit quietly and commune with God, breathe a little prayer to your guardian angel, recite our Lady's rosary, and then, instead of having wasted time, you will have saved it, the seeming misfortune of losing a train will have proved a great boon. Instead of our minds being clogged up with idle, useless, frivolous thoughts, let them be filled with some holy thoughts. The only way to preserve ourselves from sin, to make our lives pleasing to God, is to let our hearts continually send forth the sweet fragrant incense of loving prayer; I say *let* them, for they will do so of their own accord if we only give them fair play by driving away the vain and idle thoughts.

## XXX.

[There is a custom in holy homes, schools, communities, &c., of writing little practices on slips of paper, and choosing one every day or every week : we append the following.]

Resolve, when the occasion occurs, to take some affront, some injury, humbly and gently, patiently, and pray for the one who does you the wrong.

## XXXI.

Make friends with some one who does not care for you. Ask them to do some act of charity for you. This is one of the best ways of making up a quarrel, better than long explanations which do not do much good.

## XXXII.

Daily pray to our Lady to keep your *thoughts* ever in harmony with hers. Our thoughts are so exceedingly precious; and besides, they so far outnumber all the acts we can do, or words we can say.

## XXXIII.

To desire that every breath you draw should be a Spiritual Communion.

## XXXIV.

To make an act of love of Mary in union with Jesus' Heart.

## XXXV.

To make an act of love of Jesus in union with the Heart of Mary.

## XXXVI.

To repeat five times, " Jesus, meek and humble of heart, make our hearts like unto Thine."

## XXXVII.

To say often, Mother, I am thine, with all that I have.

## XXXVIII.

To repeat in honour of the five wounds, " My Jesus, mercy!" (100 days' Indulgence) for some sinner dying.

## XXXIX.

To make an act of obedience in union with Jesus.

# XL.

To practise some act of poverty for love of Jesus' poor.

# XLI.

To practise some little acts of the virtue you need most, as well as to pray for it.

# XLII.

To practise some mortification, along with a prayer for a dying sinner.

# XLIII.

To perform some hidden act of virtue purely to please God alone.

# XLIV.

To pray for all whom you have injured, in thought, word, or deed.

# XLV.

To say a "Hail Mary" often, to make up for any harm you have done.

## XLVI.

To make an intention before Office to recite the Psalms in union with our Lady, who often recited the very same.

## XLVII.

The next time you observe a fault in any one, to say a " Hail Mary" for that person, and see if you have not the same yourself.

## XLVIII.

. Say a prayer for some children who may die without Baptism if a grace is not obtained.

## XLIX.

Pray that some people who are now in the grace of God, but who might commit mortal sin and be lost, may die before that happens, if it please God.

## L.

To kiss the ground as an act of reparation to the Precious Blood that once lay dishonoured and outraged on the earth.

## LI.

To kiss the ground when you get up in the morning, in honour of your good Angel, whose feet you would wish to kiss if he were by you in visible form.

## LII.

To pray for some work, or to give some alms, promising the Guardian Angels of the people who may befriend you to say some special prayers for the good of their clients' souls.

## LIII.

To say a Magnificat and Te Deum in thanksgiving for the graces God has given you.

## LIV.

To do an act of charity to some one purely to please our Blessed Lord, who loves that, and will take what you do as done to Himself.

## LV.

To refrain from saying something you would wish to say.

## LVI.

Say a prayer for some children to be taken out of the world, who, if they grow up, may be lost.

## LVII.

Say a prayer in union with our Lady for the Church.

## LVIII.

Say a prayer for the dying, uniting your desire to our Lady's longing wish to save them.

## LIX.

Bear some little pain in union with our Blessed Lord.

## LX.

To practice some act of resignation to the Will of God.

**THE END.**

12

# CONVENT OF
# 𝕿𝖍𝖊 𝕸𝖆𝖙𝖊𝖗𝖓𝖆𝖑 𝕳𝖊𝖆𝖗𝖙 𝖔𝖋 𝕸𝖆𝖗𝖞,
## HYSON GREEN, NOTTINGHAM.

───────❈───────

The present Convent of the Maternal Heart of Mary, at Hyson Green, Nottingham, is quite inadequate to the wants of the Sisters. It consists of two poor cottages, a factory, and damp workshop. Will no one have the charity to contribute to the work of building a proper Convent, the first ever dedicated to the "*Maternal* Heart of Mary?" That sweet Mother will most certainly reward her children in the world who assist her children in the cloister.

Printed by
Richardson & Son,
Derby.

---

## Mary's Conferences to her Loving.

CHILDREN, both in the World and in the Cloister.
By the Authoress of the "Path of Mary." Post
12mo, bound in cloth, price 3s. 6d.

"We approve of the spiritual advice given in 'Mary's
Conferences,' and think it will be very profitable to those
to whom it is addressed.
"Nov. 21, 1881.    "EDWARD, BP. OF NOTTINGHAM."

"These Conferences are simple, practical, and useful. Their
special feature is the inculcation of spiritual union of life with
most holy Mary...They are full of admirable practical advice."
—*Dublin Review.*

## Mary's Call to her Loving Children;

OR, DEVOTION TO THE DYING. By the Authoress of the "Path of Mary." Post 12mo, bound
in cloth, price 2s. 6d.

"We approve of the little book entitled 'Mary's Call,
or Devotion to the Dying,' and strongly recommend it to
the faithful of our diocese.
          "EDWARD, BISHOP OF NOTTINGHAM.
"The Cathedral, Nottingham, Jan. 1, 1880."

## The Path of Mary. A new edition, with

additions. Approved by the Bishop of Nottingham. Royal 32mo, price 8d.; bound in cloth,
lettered, 1s.

"Having read several times with much pleasure and
satisfaction the little work entitled 'The Path of Mary,'
we heartily recommend it to the Faithful of our Diocese.
It appears to us to be a faithful and devout exposition of
the 'True Devotion to the Holy Virgin' of the Venerable
Grignon de Montfort, a devotion which has received the
sanction of the Church, and which is full of spiritual
graces.    "EDWARD, BISHOP OF NOTTINGHAM.
"June 24, 1878."

# RICHARDSON AND SON'S PUBLICATIONS.

## MINIATURE WORKS OF DEVOTIONAL AND PRACTICAL PIETY.

*Demy 18mo, handsomely bound in cloth, price 6d. each.*

**Communion Prayers** for every day in the week. By Canon A. O. Arvisenet.

**Heavenward.** From "Heaven Opened." By Rev. Father Collins.

**Month of Jesus Christ.** By S. Bonaventure.

**Comfort for Mourners.** By S. Francis of Sales. From his Letters. Translated by E. M. B.

**Stations of the Passion as made in Jerusalem,** and Select Devotions on the Passion, from the Prayers of S. Gertrude, O.S.B. Translated by Rev. H. Collins.

**Holy Will of God:** a Short Rule of Perfection. By the Rev. Father Benedict Canfield, Capuchin Friar. Translated by Father Collins.

**The Our Father:** Meditations on the Lord's Prayer. By St. Teresa. Translated by E. M. B.

**The Quiet of the Soul.** By Father John de Bovilla. To which is added, **Cure for Scruples.** By Dom Schram, O.S.B. Edited by the Rev. H. Collins.

**Little Manual of Direction,** for Priests, Religious Superiors, Novice-Masters and Mistresses, &c. By Dom Schram, O.S.B. Translated by Father Collins.

---

## MEDIÆVAL LIBRARY OF MYSTICAL AND ASCETICAL WORKS.

*Post 8vo, superfine cloth, lettered.*

### VOLUMES ALREADY PUBLISHED.

**Book of the Visions and Instructions of B. Angela** of Foligno, price 4s.

**The Fiery Soliloquy with God,** of Master Gerlac Petersen (Petri.) price 3s.

**Meditations on the Life and Passion of our Lord** Jesus Christ. By Dr. John Tauler. Price 6s.

**Select Revelations of St. Mechtild,** taken from the Five Books of her Spiritual Grace. Price 3s. 6d.

**Revelations of Mother Juliana,** Anchorete of Norwich. Price 4s.

# MEDITATIONS ON ALL THE MYSTERIES OF THE FAITH.

## TOGETHER

## WITH A TREATISE ON MENTAL PRAYER.

### BY THE VEN. F. LOUIS DE PONTE, S.J.

Being the translation from the Original Spanish, by J. Heigham. Revised and corrected. To which are added, the Meditations on the Sacred Heart of Jesus. By the Ven. F. C. Borgo, S.J. Translated into English. The last volume contains a copious and valuable analytical Index to the whole. Complete in six vols. post 8vo., superfine paper, printed wrapper, price 18s.

The complete set (6 vols.) strongly bound in dark cloth, red edges, lettered, £1. 10s.— Calf, or morocco plain, gilt or red edges, price £2. 8s.—Morocco extra, gilt or red edges, £3. 12s.—Super calf, or morocco plain, bevelled boards, extra strong, gilt or red edges, price £3. 12s.—Morocco super extra, price £4. 4s.

Any Volume may be had separately.

---

## CONTENTS OF THE SIX VOLUMES.

VOL. I.—INTRODUCTION, On Mental Prayer.—MEDITATIONS on the Mysteries of our holy Faith.—I. For Beginners in the Purgative Way.—INTRODUCTION, On Purity, which is the end of the Purgative Way. —MEDITATIONS. 1, On Sins; 2, On the last Things of Man; 3, Others, with forms of prayer in order to the mortification of the vices; 4, preparatory to Confession and Communion.

VOL. II.—II. For Proficients in the Illuminative Way, —INTRODUCTION.—On the perfect imitation of our Saviour Christ.—MEDITATIONS on the Mysteries of the Incarnation and Infancy of our Lord Jesus Christ until His Baptism.

APPENDIX, Fr. C. Borgo's Meditations on the Sacred Heart.

VOL. III.—INTRODUCTION—On the Active, Contemplative, and Mixed kinds of Life.—MEDITATIONS on the chief Mysteries of our Lord's Life, teaching, and miracles, up to the end of His preaching.

VOL. IV.—INTRODUCTION.—On Mental Prayer, on the Passion of our Saviour Jesus Christ.—MEDITATIONS on the Mysteries of the whole Passion.

VOL. V.—III. For the Perfect in the Unitive Way.—INTRODUCTION. On Union with God the end of the Unitive Way.—MEDITATIONS on the Mysteries of our Lord's Resurrection, appearances, and Ascension, up to the Coming of the Holy Ghost and the promulgation of the Gospel.

VOL. VI.—INTRODUCTION.—On fervent affections of Love and Thanksgiving.—MEDITATIONS on the Mysteries of the Divinity, Trinity, attributes and perfections of God; and the benefits, natural and supernatural, flowing from Him.

---

## Life of the Venerable Louis de Ponte

S.J., uniform with the above, paper wrapper, price 3s.; dark cloth, red edges, price 5s.; extra cloth, blocked black, gold lettering, price 4s.

## Life of Father Balthasar Alvarez, religious of the Society of Jesus. By the Venerable Louis de Ponte, S.J. Complete in two volumes, post 8vo, price 7s.

## Father Milleriot, the Ravignan of the WORKING MEN OF PARIS. From the French of the Rev. Pere Clair, S.J., with the special permission of the Author. By Mrs. F. Raymond-Barker. Foolscap 8vo, extra cloth, blocked black, lettered in gold, price 2s.

## Spiritual Letters of Father Surin, S.J.

First Series. Translated by Sister M. Christopher, Order of St. Francis. With a Preface by Father Francis Goldie, S.J. Edited by the Rev. H. Collins. Price 4s. 6d.

## The Life of Dom Bartholomew of the

MARTYRS, Religious of the Order of St. Dominic, Archbishop of Braga, in Portugal. Translated from his Biographies. By Lady Herbert. Demy 8vo, extra cloth, price 12s. 6d.

## Heaven Opened; or our Home in

HEAVEN AND THE WAY THITHER. A Manual of Guidance for Devout Souls. By Rev. Father Collins. Post 8vo, handsomely bound, price 5s.

## Bernadette. — Sister Marie-Bernard.

The Sequel to "Our Lady of Lourdes." By Henri Lasserre. Translated with the special permission of the author, by Mrs. F. Raymond-Barker. Foolscap 8vo, ornamental cloth, price 4s.

## Francis Willington; or a Life for the

FOREIGN MISSIONS. By Weston Reay. With Preface by Rev. Isaac Moore, S.J. Dedicated by permission to His Lordship the Bishop of Salford. Crown 8vo, elegantly bound in cloth, price 5s.

## Primacy of St. Peter demonstrated

from the Liturgy of the Greco-Russian Church. With an Appendix containing several Documents and the Russian Text of all the passages quoted from the Slavonic Liturgy. By the Rev. C. Tondini de Quarenghi, Barnabite. Demy 8vo, price 3s.

## Complin; Benediction; Quarant' Ore;

with a Selection of Psalms and Hymns. Extra cloth, gold lettering, red edges, price 1s.

## Cash Book, for Public Institutions, Schools,

Societies, and General Commercial Purposes.

Oblong 6to, large post, full cloth, lettered on side in gold, red edges, price 1s. 4d.
Ditto, strong leather back, cloth sides, lettered in gold, red edges, price 2s.
Quarto, large post, full cloth, lettered on side in gold, red edges, price 1s. 6d.
Ditto, strong leather back, cloth sides, lettered in gold, red edges, price 2s. 6d.

RICHARDSON AND SON'S PUBLICATIONS.

## The Problem Solved. Edited by Lady
Herbert. Crown 8vo, 450 pp., extra cloth, blocked black, with gold lettering, price 6s.

## Virgin Mary according to the Gospel.
Edited by the Rev. H. Collins. Post 8vo, superfine cloth, price 6s. 6d.

## Nun of the Order of the Visitation,
ANNE MADELEINE DE REMUSAT, of Marseilles, called the Second Margaret Mary of the Sacred Heart. Foolscap 8vo, superfine cloth, price 3s. 6d.

## Graziella; or the History of a Broken
HEART. An Episode of my Life. By A. De Lamartine. Translated from the French by J. B. S. Foolscap 8vo, cloth elegant, 2s. 6d.

## Lights and Shadows of Home Affections.
A Moral Tale for the present epoch. Humbly Dedicated to her virtuous Queen, by the authoress of " Footsteps through Life," " Geraldine," &c. Crown 8vo, elegantly bound in cloth, price 7s.

## Lectures on Catholic Faith and Practice.
By the Right Rev. J. N. Sweeney, O.S.B. Complete in three vols., price 9s.

## Manual of Devotion to the Sacred Heart
OF JESUS. By the Rev. Father Gautrelet, S.J. Translated from the French. A NEW EDITION, *considerably enlarged, containing all the approved popular Devotions to the Sacred Heart.* Cheap edition, price 2s.—Superfine cloth, lettered, price 3s.

## Month of the Sacred Heart of Jesus.
Translated from the French by the Rev. George Tickell, S.J. Post 12mo, superfine cloth, lettered, price 2s.

## Life and Select Writings of the Venerable Louis Maria Grignon de Montfort.
Translated by a Secular Priest of the Third Order of St. Dominic. Post 8vo, price 5s.

www.ingramcontent.com/pod-product-compliance
Lightning Source LLC
Chambersburg PA
CBHW020851020726
47497CB00005B/1353